hed Fate

wope

&

Genilee Swope Parente

Wretched Fate

This novel is a work of fiction. Any references to real people, events, establishments, organizations, or locales are intended only to give the fiction a sense of reality and authenticity, and are used fictitiously.

All other names, characters, and places, and all dialogue and incidents portrayed in this book are the product of the author's imagination.

An e-book edition of this book was published in 2013 by Spectacle Publishing Media Group, LLC.

WRETCHED FATE.

First Edition.

For information address:

Spectacle Publishing Media Group
P.O. Box 295,
Lisle, NY 13797

Cover design by Rob Gee
Author Photo by Aleda Johnson Powell

ISBN 978-1938444074

Acknowledgements

We learned quickly, after having our first book ***Twist of Fate*** published, who the real heroes for writers are: our readers. Getting published is not an easy or profitable venture for most authors, especially with a first effort. However, the hundreds of encouraging comments we got from individuals made it well worth the hours spent fine-tuning the plot and making our characters come to life. They are the reason this sequel, and those to come, will be successful. From Verna Wortkoetter—a long-time family friend who takes the time to write and keep us going—to our blog readers, to the many good people in our hometown of Edgerton, Ohio who emailed and wrote to tell us how much they enjoyed our first book, you are our inspiration.

As always, author Allyn Stotz has been our number one cheerleader, and we hope she'll continue to feed the fire that keeps us going. We once again benefitted from the research expertise of Mark Swope, who made sure we were accurate about some of our facts. Elvis Bello, a former detective in the Richmond Metro Area and a current investigator in the Northern Virginia area, let us run some of our criminal ideas by him. Dr. Frank P. Ciampi, family physician of the Williamsburg Square Family Medical Practice in Lorton, Virginia, took the time to listen to ideas about illnesses and proper responses. If there are mistakes in the plot of ***Wretched Fate***, they occurred after we consulted with these people.

We want to acknowledge that, once again, we are grateful to the people at Spectacle Media Publishing Group who shared with us their editing and publishing expertise and gave both guidance and encouragement. With this book, we especially want to thank Angi Gray for heading up the editorial team who gave the book the spit and shine it needed.

We also would like to thank Bob Swope, who has chauffeured us around to various communities for book signings, and Ray Parente, who joined Bob in trying to understand why his wife spends so many hours at the keyboard. Without the love and support of our spouses and families, we couldn't do what we do.

Finally, we want to thank every one of the people at those signings and book club events who approached us to tell us we are lucky to do what we do or that they loved our first book. We're pretty sure you'll enjoy this second one even more.

Genilee Parente & Sharon Swope-Parente

Table of Contents

Prologue 5
Chapter 1 9
Chapter 2 15
Chapter 3 21
Chapter 4 29
Chapter 5 39
Chapter 6 43
Chapter 7 47
Chapter 8 55
Chapter 9 64
Chapter 10 71
Chapter 11 77
Chapter 12 83
Chapter 13 87
Chapter 14 95
Chapter 15 101
Chapter 16 109
Chapter 17 115
Chapter 18 121
Chapter 19 127
Chapter 20 135
Chapter 21 141
Chapter 22 149
Chapter 23 163
Chapter 24 173
Chapter 25 183
Chapter 26 191
Chapter 27 197
Chapter 28 201
Chapter 29 209
Chapter 30 217
Chapter 31 225
Chapter 32 233
Chapter 33 239
Chapter 34 247
Chapter 35 253
Chapter 36 259
Chapter 37 263
Epilogue 271

Prologue

A small boy sat quietly on the high-backed chair, his feet not reaching the floor. His posture was rigid, his face blank, as a woman in a white uniform attended to his bleeding knee. She dabbed very gently at the wound.

"There," Nurse Roberts said. "I think we have all the gravel out." Her warm and friendly smile went unreturned. Sighing, the nurse took a tube from the table beside them. "This may hurt just a little, but the medicine will prevent infection."

The child remained silent as a tear welled in his eye.

Nurse Roberts unwrapped a large Band-Aid and covered his scrape, and then placed a hand lightly on the small boy's head. "Thank you for being such a brave little man. I think we have your knee all taken care of for now, but it was a pretty bad scrape. We should call your parents and see if they want to come get you and take you to a doctor."

The boy jerked his head upward to look at the nurse's face, knocking her hand from its resting place. "No!" he cried. "Don't call them!" His head dropped back down, and he took a deep breath to calm himself. "It doesn't hurt," the boy said softly. "I don't need to go to a doctor."

Nurse Roberts' brow wrinkled. She returned

her hand to his head and patted gently, her voice touched with tenderness. "I can't make that decision," she said. "But if you really want to stay in school and your knee doesn't hurt, I'll check with Principal Stevens. Stay here, and I'll be right back."

The boy sat stiffly, his face stoic, lips pressed tightly together even as a tear finally spilled. He wiped it away quickly.

Principal Stevens, a lanky man with broad shoulders, entered the room trailed by the nurse. He settled his tall frame into the chair facing the small boy.

"Nurse Roberts thinks you probably should go home after such a fall and maybe have a doctor check you out. You hit your head when you went down."

"No, please," the boy said, his voice barely a whisper. "It was just a little bump." He didn't meet the older man's eyes. Like most students at the school, the boy respected the principal, who made the children feel important by listening carefully to what they said before any scolding or warning. Principal Stevens waited until the silence caused the boy to look up.

"Your parents might be angry with us if we don't send you home. I know this is the first week of school, and I'm glad you like your teacher and classroom, but there will be many more days of school to come."

"I don't need to go home, Sir," the boy said, his voice now steady and calm. "And my parents will be upset with me."

"Everyone has accidents once in a while. Why would they be upset?" the principal asked, but he noticed the boy peering out the window.

"I want to stay. My knee and my head don't hurt." The urge to cry won and tears fell softly on the small boy's lap.

Principal Stevens noticed, but didn't comment. "I know you want to be courageous, but I'm sure your parents would rather have you home."

The tears became sobs. The boy was now breathing heavily.

"They won't let me come back," he cried. "I want to go to school. Please."

The principal drew back in his chair and looked over at the nurse, a question in his eyes.

"Why wouldn't you want to go home, young man?"

As quickly as the crying began, it stopped. The boy brushed the tears away, took a big breath, let his eyes wander the room, and then find their way back to the principal's face.

"I made a friend in class," the boy confided. "The girl with curly hair and the pretty polka dot dress. She said she'd be my friend after the other kids made fun of my clothes. I never had a friend like her. Can I please stay in school today and play with her?"

"We'll let your parents decide when we call them, Son," Principal Stevens said. "If they say okay, we'll send a report home on what happened, and the nurse can check on your knee tomorrow. Okay?"

The little boy looked up at the man, his eyes holding no joy.

"Okay."

But that was the last day anyone in school saw the little boy.

Chapter 1

Sam Osborne relished the feel of steaming hot water on his tired muscles after his morning exercise routine. He wasn't a fitness nut, but he made sure that his five-foot-six frame stayed in good shape. Although he was a private investigator, he hated carrying a gun. He knew he at least needed the capability to defend himself against the occasional belligerent person, so he kept up the regimen he began many years ago when he was on the police force. Now, at fifty-two, his body was softly rippled with muscle and lacked the usual tire around the middle that most men his age carried.

He stood in steamy water letting his muscles relax. Eventually, he turned off the water, grabbed a thick towel, and dried himself.

Facing the mirror, he picked up a comb to try to put his thick brown hair into place. One strand fought his ministrations and fell loose over his forehead. Sam smiled at the errant curl.

He yawned, cocked his head, buttoned the last button of his soft blue cotton shirt, and picked up his sports jacket on the way out the door.

All in all, Sam was satisfied with his life. He'd traveled a rocky road for so many years—losing his son, going through a divorce, and more recently, losing his dog Buddy, who had finally succumbed to old age. Just to have the detective business running smoothly felt deeply satisfying. Sam knew that despite the bumps of life, he was lucky. He didn't work for money. Sam had not needed to support himself since his father passed away and left him a small fortune. Being idle would have killed a man used to police work, and idleness didn't sit well with him. His mind craved puzzles, and his body was always ready for the next challenge. These days, Sam took the cases he wanted, and left plenty of time for other activities, such as meeting up with his old friends on the force. Occasionally, he headed out of town with a fishing pole.

Sam went downstairs to his newly remodeled office space to greet the person largely responsible for developing a system to keep the detective operation running smoothly. His secretary, Casey Jones, was blond and beautiful, but Sam didn't hire her for that reason. He'd helped Casey with her own case, and then hired her when he realized how bright she was.

Except for a few boxes from his old office yet to be unpacked, the remodeling move was almost complete. It had been well worth the expense and effort. He'd transferred from a downtown office—a cramped second-story space—to his own home in order to create a warmer, more familiar environment. He also had the space reconfigured to accommodate Casey's wheelchair.

As always, Casey's smile was like popping a fresh mint in his mouth; her sunny disposition refreshed him.

"Sam. Good morning!" she said, pushing her silky tresses back from her face. "Coffee?"

"Of course."

"I have maple glazed donuts from Mabel's."

"Look, Casey. You've only been back from maternity leave for a month. Are you shooting for a raise already or just trying to fatten me up?"

Casey laughed heartily, and the sound reminded Sam of a summer wind chime. He was so glad she and her husband, Danny, had come into his life.

"How's little Gus this morning?" Sam asked as he took a big bite from the delicacy Casey offered.

Her smile turned into a yawn. "Oh, he was fine when I left, but he sure wasn't fine most of the night. He kept Danny and me hopping with his fussing. I suppose he'll sleep like a charm for Sarah this morning."

Sam took another small bite. "I'm sure Sarah will know how to handle him. She raised you, after all."

Casey nodded slowly, her far-off gaze revealing to Sam that his secretary's mind was still at home. Sam saw when her thoughts returned to the office and her job; she squared her shoulders and looked around her desk until she located a note.

"Shawn Dougherty called early this morning to tell you she's meeting up with her mom," Casey said. "She wanted to express her gratitude again for your help in putting the two of them together."

"I hope it goes well with them. Just because they are related by blood doesn't mean they'll get along ..."

His voice faded as he went into his own office and sat down behind his thick wooden desk.

Casey wheeled in after him, a pile of papers on her lap. She lifted them off her chair and put them on the edge of his desk, retaining just the top sheet.

"I finished up the reports, Sam. Time to take this check to the bank."

Casey turned her chair to leave, but turned it back around again. "Oh, and you probably have a new client."

"Probably?" Sam asked, his nose in the reports he was flipping through.

Casey's eyes twinkled. "It really seemed like a Sam Osborne case to me."

Sam's gaze rose slowly from the papers to meet his secretary's green orbs. "Okay, spill it."

"It seems that a rich and famous author has some valuable statuettes that keep disappearing from his mansion. His very secure mansion. His extremely locked up house that no one goes into except one long-time servant and the author's agent. There have been four robberies in four months and he's distraught about the disappearances. He's filed a police report, but it's not exactly a priority at headquarters."

"Okay, you've piqued my interest. What time is he coming into the office?"

Casey turned back towards the door and began wheeling out, calling over her shoulder, "Oh, he's not coming in. Doesn't like to leave the mansion if he can help it. He wants you to go meet with him at two. I took the liberty of agreeing." She chuckles softly. "Like I said, sounds like a Sam Osborne case."

Chapter 2

Rosalie McGovern stood naked in front of her bedroom mirror. She tried hard not to grimace as she peered into the glass. The magazine article insisted this exercise was a basis for self-growth. She was supposed to remove all outside adornment, study her full image in the mirror, and visualize her body as an extension of her inner beauty.

"You must learn to love your own shape and accept it as a part of you," Rosalie read, "because no one else will accept you, if you don't accept yourself." She leaned toward the mirror.

Sure, of course. But that doesn't make it any easier to face this mirror. And it doesn't make the extra flesh go away either.

She glanced back at the magazine.

"Take your breasts in your hands. Feel how soft and full they are," Rosalie read. She slammed the magazine face down in disgust.

"I'm not a fool, and I'm not a pervert," she said to her image, shaking her finger at the mirror. "My breasts are nice and full, but they are too big. My nipples aren't rosy pink like the heroines' in novels. They're light brown and dimply."

Determined to try a more positive approach, she sighed and ran her hands slowly down her sides as the magazine had instructed. The lumps and bulges she felt towards the middle stopped her, and she finally hung her head in frustration. Abruptly, her head snapped up and her eyes blazed.

"Bloody hell! No article is going to change the fact that I'm fat!" she spat at her reflection and then threw the magazine across the room.

This is silly and useless. I am what I am.

Rosalie had tried every diet she'd ever heard about; despite that, the scales rarely budged below one hundred sixty-five pounds. She knew some women might be pleased with that consistency—especially if they were five inches taller than her five-foot-three. But Rosalie wanted to look more like the women in the magazines and less like a Rubenesque statue with a boob job.

She walked away from the mirror, picked up clothes from the bed and dressed.

Back at the mirror, Rosalie ran her hands through her curly black hair, which by luck was always lustrous, full and shiny. She also knew her eyes, a deep rich green, were her best feature. She was often teased about how cute her petite little ears were, and they went along well with her small wrists and ankles.

Now all I need to do is find a man interested in tiny parts on an overweight woman. The thought finally made her laugh.

At forty-two, Rosalie knew it was time to put away dreams of a husband and children. She hadn't dated much in the last five years, though she'd certainly had her share of dates in her thirties. Her small circle of friends, while supportive and encouraging, no longer even bothered fixing her up with blind dates—her attitude was too negative, they said. Rosalie hated forced conversation, and most men wanted only to talk about themselves. She was intelligent, well read, and usually happiest behind a book. She preferred talking with her friends about the complexities of plot twists, rather than sharing an awkward dinner with an eligible bachelor who wanted to discuss how difficult it was being a claims adjuster.

She couldn't really share stories about her career since it had never taken off. Rosalie had gone to business school, but the only part of what she studied that seemed natural to her was typing. She hated accounting and budgets, didn't want to be anyone's boss, and also didn't particularly care how a company marketed its products.

She was organized and efficient. Thirty years earlier, she would have been well-qualified and happy as a secretary. But today's business world had evolved into one run by computers and marketing concepts, and while her fingers flew over a keyboard at ninety words a minute, she did not get along with technology in general. Her attempts at being a receptionist had failed; she recognized right away that she didn't have the ability to multi-task on the complicated phone system.

Finally, she gave up the world of offices and tried regular college. She'd loved every minute of every English class she had taken and was excited about the prospect of sharing her thoughts through teaching. She hadn't been able to afford more than a couple of years though, and a half-way-there degree in education had done her no good. Between stints with a temp agency that had recently shut its doors, she'd found work as a substitute teacher. However, subbing wasn't a full-time job, and she was tired of moving back home when the money ran out.

So here she was, staring into the mirror: forty-two, unmarried, unemployed (again), and living with a mother who treated her like a lost cause.

Rosalie bent over, picked up the magazine, and placed it on her nightstand while admonishing herself for reading such a silly article in the first place. She went into the kitchen to fix herself eggs and bacon. *At least "Dear Old Mom" is off with the church ladies and won't try to feed me even more*, she thought as she impulsively topped off her plate with a cinnamon roll and went into the living room to sit on the sofa.

Sighing heavily, she picked up the employment section of the Sunday newspaper.

I better look. Unemployment runs out in a couple of weeks.

She opened the paper and took a huge bite of her sweet treat. She ran one finger down the page, not really feeling any hope.

Suddenly, her finger stopped on an ad. She couldn't believe what she read.

"Wanted: typist willing to work with a Dictaphone and typewriter. No computer skills required.

Will work in my home transcribing tapes for a fiction book. J.H., 4900 Peacock Lane. Interviews Monday thru Wednesday, 3:00 – 4:30 p.m."

"Could it be that simple?" she said aloud. "What's the catch?" She closed the paper and sat there for a few minutes.

"Oh, what the hell. See you at three."

Chapter 3

Jacob Hardy ate his usual breakfast of one boiled egg and one piece of whole-wheat toast with a light layer of butter at precisely six thirty a.m. He opened his paper and took out the sports section, folded it, and laid it aside to read later and compare statistics against what the television sports announcers had to say.

Few people who had met Jacob Hardy would have believed what the man did for a living if they hadn't known beforehand. In person, he looked much more like a lawyer or a CPA than a romance novelist. He was always formally dressed and immaculate, though he left his suit coat hanging in the closet when he was at home. His appearance did not hint at his uncanny ability to write novels that women devoured with the same hunger they had for chocolates—his words were caloric, but irresistible.

There weren't many people who knew what the author's daily life was like. Jacob had no friends and had been turning down social invitations for years. He lived in a mansion by himself and only rarely had visitors. Most people would label him a recluse. He didn't mind and was used to his aloneness—he'd never really had many people in his life. And while the romance novels Jacob wrote made his name famous, he didn't even allow his picture on the book cover.

Jacob liked it that way. He had no use for the silliness and attention that fame brought. He certainly had no use for the hundreds of enamored women who wrote flowery letters to the man whose stories made their hearts flutter.

Jacob had never married; he'd dated in his twenties and hired companions in his thirties when he was still attending a few social events. Now in his forties, he finally settled for visiting a discreet local prostitute once or twice a month.

Jacob Hardy had been brought up in a house with no love and could see no purpose behind pursuing the opposite sex except for physical release and book research. In fact, he believed that not being tied down by marriage, or needing to pursue relationships, helped his writing. It gave him the freedom to write romances that appealed to those that were caught in the constraints of everyday obligations.

The books had made him millions, but since he didn't need or want those millions, few people would understand why he continued to write. They would not understand how fully Jacob had compartmentalized his life. A "real" world existed in routine and neatness; Jacob lived in the gilded cage of this real world, protected by his money and his schedules. Within its bounds, he was free to live an imaginary life rich with desire, fantasy, and boiling emotions.

Jacob couldn't explain the source of his ideas, and the media had long ago given up trying to get interviews. Most didn't care anymore. His books lived short lives on the "best selling romances" shelf and then were filed away on the back shelves where fans knew to find them.

No one knew that Jacob's passion was not in the printed product itself, but rather in the method of creation. His words sprang from something deep inside himself and were beautifully put together, though his plots and characters were predictable.

Jacob seldom smiled and seldom became angry. In fact, he was very much like one of the statues he collected—cold to the touch but beautiful in appearance.

His height, slenderness and fine-boned face drew the eyes of both women and men. Although he was in his mid-forties, he looked much younger when he wasn't frowning or when his features weren't pinched from deep thinking.

At this moment, he was definitely frowning as he hung up the phone. He'd been talking to his agent Malcolm Sherburne who, once again, had insisted Jacob find a more efficient way to produce his manuscripts. A few years ago, Malcolm had encouraged his bestselling author to come into the modern realm of technology.

Jacob had given the computer a chance. He'd purchased the latest and greatest laptop and had a few dreadful hours with an instructor. He'd then spent a few days trying to put the lessons into practice. However, it hadn't been long before Jacob banished the machine to the attic because it ate four hours of his work. That kind of destruction and schedule interruption was not acceptable to Jacob. Besides, he knew the agent's insistence on the computer was more for the ability to crank out manuscripts than for Jacob's convenience.

He'd locked the machine away and announced to Malcolm that he was back to pencil and pad, his trusty voice recorder, which had helped him work out many ideas, and the hunt-and-peck of typing them out onto paper.

Malcolm was not pleased and had convinced Jacob to try using a Dictaphone and typist. What the agent hadn't told him until this morning was that the interviews started that very day, just an hour after Jacob had arranged his meeting with a detective. The afternoon would be wasted.

***

Jacob spent the rest of that morning in his study working until exactly twelve o'clock, when he took thirty minutes to eat a lunch of chicken salad and a muffin that his housekeeper Mrs. Wells had left in the kitchen. He continued working until two p.m., when the alarm on his wristwatch went off. He lifted his head just as he heard the doorbell clang.

A rare smile flashed across his face. "Right on time," he whispered.

Jacob answered the door himself, because Mrs. Wells did not live in the house with him; she lived on the grounds in her own home. Despite the size of Jacob's mansion, he wanted no one else around when he was in the throes of writing.

"Mr. Osborne, I presume." Jacob shook Sam's hand and then gestured for the detective to follow. In a nearby sitting room, Jacob indicated chairs where they could both sit comfortably.

The difference between Sam, whom many considered a soft-spoken man, and Jacob, who was silent most of the time, was evident in the twinkle and liveliness of Sam's hazel eyes. Those eyes now wandered the room, taking in the richness and tastefulness of the furnishings. Jacob had long ago stopped seeing the details of any room in his home.

"Thank you for calling my office and setting this meeting up," Sam began. "How can we help? I believe my assistant said something about the theft of some valuable statuettes?"

Jacob sat with his fingers intertwined, his joined hands resting on one knee.

"Someone has been stealing my Oriental figurines, Mr. Osborne. Right from under my nose," he said. "I cannot imagine who or how this is being done. I am rarely gone from the house, and I believe the thefts are occurring at night while I'm sleeping. I have no staff except Mrs. Wells, who brings in my meals and cleans the house twice a week. Even she doesn't have keys."

Sam opened his notebook and began to take notes. "What do the police say?"

"I contacted the police after I found the first one missing and filed reports as the next three disappeared, but I suppose they have better things to do than to find a wealthy man's possessions. My insurance company is concerned about how they have gone missing right from under my nose, but they haven't yet questioned my reports or been out to investigate. I brought you in because I need to get to the bottom of this."

Sam looked up at Jacob. "Who else has access to this house, Mr. Hardy, besides Mrs. Wells?"

"There's an outside employee—Horace Montgomery—who cuts my grass and takes cares of the shrubs. But he comes inside only rarely, to discuss schedules. My publisher, Malcolm Sherburne, is a frequent visitor, but he has no reason I can think of to steal my statues. I've made him a wealthy man. Neither of these men have keys to my house. I just can't understand what is going on."

Sam noted the wrinkled brow and drumming fingers of the man sitting in the other armchair. The statues were obviously of great importance to the author. Sam tried smiling to put Jacob at ease with no effect. He looked back down at his notebook and scribbled.

"Perhaps you could tell me more about the statues, so I know what I'm looking for."

Jacob cleared his throat. "Of course. They are more statuettes than statues. Most of them were produced some time during the Ming Dynasty by various artists. They feature Kuan Yin, the Goddess of Mercy."

Jacob rose and went to a nearby desk, picking up a stack of papers.

"I have pictures of them that you can take with you. I get them from a shop in Hope, Pennsylvania, run by Gregory Sterling. I've written down the number here and included copies of receipts from the shop. He can tell you more about them."

Sam's eyes wandered the room again and then returned to the notebook. "I'll need to look around your home to see if I can spot any signs of someone breaking in," Sam said. "I'll talk to your housekeeper, the gardener and Mr. Sterling." When Sam's head came up again, he saw Jacob still standing at the desk with papers in hand, looking nervously at the clock.

"Yes, that makes sense, but not today, I'm afraid. I'm sorry to cut this visit short, but my publisher insisted I interview typists. He put an ad in yesterday's paper and didn't tell me until this morning. Anyway, I need to prepare for the interviewing, which begins in less than an hour. Can your investigation start tomorrow?"

"Of course," Sam said. He stood and took the papers from Jacob. "I'm in the middle of moving my office and can use the extra time. We should be finished with most of the boxes by tomorrow.

"I wish you luck on your interviews, though," Sam added. "I was lucky to find my assistant. But I know how tough interviewing can be."

"I wouldn't know," Jacob responded. He nervously ran his hand back and forth across the top of one of the chairs. Jacob's next words were said so softly, Sam was sure they weren't intended for his ears. "I wouldn't be doing this, if not forced into it."

Jacob seemed to realize that he was muttering then and withdrew his hand from the back of the chair. He straightened his shoulders and held out his hand for a formal shake. "Thank you for coming, Mr. Osborne. Tomorrow at eleven?"

"Eleven it is," Sam replied. "In the meantime, try to think in terms of how someone might get into this house. Even if they don't have a key, there has to be a way."

Chapter 4

Rosalie tore at the buttons, took off her dress and threw it on the bed in a crumpled mess. She had just tried on her fourth outfit. She knew she had to choose one quickly; her mother had already called up twice for Rosalie to come down for lunch. Rosalie tried to explain to Mom that her nerves would not allow her to eat. As usual, Mom was so focused on fulfilling her idea of what a mother should do, that she had not listened to her daughter.

"You have to eat some lunch," Doris McGovern called up the steps. "It's almost two o'clock. If you don't eat, how can you get a good start on your new job?"

"It's not a job yet, Mom," Rosalie yelled loudly down the steps, but she immediately felt guilty at her impatience. Taking her nervousness out on her mother was childish. "Okay, Mom. I'll be down in a sec. But just some fruit and a glass of milk."

She picked up the first skirt she had tried on, deciding it would have to do. Rosalie's instincts told her not to be late for this interview.

She slid the black skirt over her head and reached for the matching black, button-front tunic. At least the outfit was full and covered most of her body. It was drab and did nothing for her complexion, but it was professional-looking.

"I'm definitely not a 'black' person," she said out loud as she peered into the mirror. Fastening silver hoops into her ears and encircling her wrist with a matching silver bracelet, she grabbed her purse and tore down the steps, hoping to grab the fruit on her way out the door.

Instead, Doris stood at the table holding a plate of two grilled cheese sandwiches and a pile of potato chips.

Rosalie groaned inwardly. "I can't eat, Mother, really. I'm going to be late." Despite protesting, she sat down at the table as her mother plopped the plate down.

I've been a woman for a lot more years than you stayed married. You know I want to lose weight, but you insist on another heaping plate of food. Rosalie sighed deeply.

"Is *that* what you're wearing for your interview?" Doris said. "It's so drab, dear, but I guess it hides those bulges."

Her comment pushed Rosalie from annoyance to anger. She pushed her plate back and stood, leaving most of the sandwiches and all the chips.

"I'm sorry, Mother. I cannot be late."

"I went to all that work…" Doris' voice followed Rosalie out the door.

The taxi was just pulling up at the curb. The cab had been a splurge, but Rosalie felt it was better to arrive that way than to walk the distance and arrive sweating, and she didn't want to be delivered by a mother that would probably insist on coming inside.

In the cab, Rosalie took deep, calming breaths. When the car pulled up in front of a mansion, Rosalie's nervousness turned into shock. She opened the door and got out, pulling a twenty from her purse without even looking at it and handed it to the driver. Realizing that the fare could not be that much, she turned back, thanked the driver, and got her change.

After the taxi pulled away, Rosalie stood on the sidewalk gazing up at the place. The home took up half a block and stood three stories high. Ivy climbed up the exterior brick walls. Carefully trimmed shrubs adorned both sides of the driveway and circled the house. Flowers bloomed everywhere. Although the sheer size of the building was imposing, the soft fragrance of the flowers and the green vines and leaves softened the effect.

Rosalie wasn't certain if it was the house or just her nerves, but she was trembling. It didn't matter how she felt, though. She was determined to go through with the interview. She straightened her purse strap on her shoulder, adjusted her skirt so the seams were in place, and walked up to the front door.

Rosalie knocked on the huge ornate oak door, expecting to see a butler. When it creaked open, however, the man who answered was not dressed in a uniform. Rosalie observed grey chino pants and a crisply ironed white shirt. He waved a hand to usher her in, then turned his back and began walking away. He had barely looked her way, and he hadn't smiled.

Rosalie and the man arrived at a door. He turned towards Rosalie, indicating that she should enter. He still hadn't said a word.

Once inside the cavernous room, Rosalie's nervousness increased. Three other applicants sat on wing-backed chairs, leaving a brocade couch open. Rosalie took a seat on the couch, looked around at the other women, and swallowed. She could see she faced stiff competition. Two of the women were at least ten years younger than she. They were dressed in expensive-looking, tailored suits and wore self-confidence on their expertly made-up faces. The third woman was older than Rosalie and matronly, both in the flowery dress she wore and the warm smile on her face.

The smile didn't make Rosalie feel any better. This was a small crowd compared to most interviews Rosalie had been through, probably because of the mention of a typewriter instead of a computer. But she doubted she stood a chance next to two attractive go-getters and one woman who likely had years more experience.

After only a few minutes, the man returned to the entrance of the room and Rosalie heard the front door open and close. *Another applicant must be leaving already*, she thought. Rosalie looked at her watch and realized that while she had made it in time, the other four had been early.

Rosalie studied the man who now stood just inside the door of the room. He was tall and thin and would have been attractive if not for his pinched expression. He stood stiffly, a pencil behind one ear, a pad of paper in his hand, and a deep frown on his face. The man called out the name of one of the other ladies. A petite blond with a short skirt stood up and followed him out of the room. Not even five minutes later, the front door slammed, and the thin man again stood at the room's entrance.

"I can't do this today, ladies. I'm sorry. No more interviews." He seemed to realize how blunt he sounded and added, "Thank you for coming," before gesturing towards the front doorway. He then retreated back down the hall.

Rosalie remained seated, stunned at the interviewer's rudeness, while the other women stomped out, grumbling. Though she hadn't expected to get the job, she was angry. After all her worrying, putting on makeup, choosing an outfit, paying for a cab, and practically fighting with her mom over lunch, she felt cheated. She crossed her arms and sat back on the sofa—dark storm clouds gathering in her brain.

Who the hell does he think he is? He puts the ad in the paper, and then on a whim, decides he doesn't feel like interviewing today?

***

Jacob was back in his beloved study sitting at his big cherry desk. He put his hands behind his head and heaved a giant sigh of relief. Leaning forward, he began to go through the notes he'd started early in the day. It was several moments before he looked up and saw through the open door that one of the women had not left. She was standing just inside his study door, her purse on her shoulder, her back against the doorframe.

"The interviews are over!" Jacob said firmly.

"No," Rosalie said, acid in her voice. "The interviews most certainly are not over. You said you were interviewing from three to four-thirty. It is now three twenty-three. That means the interviews have only just begun. I am ready for my interview."

Jacob stared at the woman, his mouth agape. He wondered if he should be alarmed, but she didn't really look dangerous, just angry.

As she walked up to his desk, Jacob's eyes traveled from her neatly pulled back raven hair, to her curvy figure, then back up to bright green eyes that seemed to pop and crackle.

She looks like one of the heroines from my books.

He knew she was justified in her anger. Malcolm had been wrong to force the issue. But Jacob shouldn't have let his irritation with the situation and his nervousness with interviewing get in the way, even if two of the interviewees looked and sounded like spoiled teenagers.

He sighed deeply and sat back to continue his perusal of the raging woman in front of him. She was about the same age as him, dressed neatly and plainly in a dark outfit. He probably wouldn't have noticed her on the street unless she was in a volatile mood. He didn't ask her to sit.

"Can you type?" he asked.

"Ninety words a minute," she replied. "I have

never used a Dictaphone, but I know I can handle it."

Rosalie hung her head briefly then, as if getting her emotions under control. When her head came back up, she confessed, "I'm afraid computers don't seem to care for me, however."

The corners of Jacob's mouth rose. That hint of a smile transformed his face from icy to approachable. His voice was much softer as he said, "I tried to use one myself, but that damn computer hated me. How's your spelling?"

Rosalie's stiff posture relaxed. "Not perfect. Better than most. And I usually know when something isn't right. I know how to use a dictionary."

"You're comfortable then with a typewriter, instead of a keyboard?"

"I very much prefer the rhythm of the keys, to the sound of myself cussing at the computer," Rosalie replied.

Jacob actually laughed then. He still had not asked her to sit. Standing up, he sobered quickly and said, "Leave your resume and references on my desk. If I find nothing amiss, the job is yours. Come back in two days if I haven't called you. That will give me a day to record some thoughts. Your hours are nine to twelve and one to five, unless I have business outside the office or something besides writing to do. Oh," he said as he peered more closely at her face, "there are explicit sex scenes in my books. Will that bother you?"

"No, sir, I'm fine with that," Rosalie answered

politely.

"Good." Jacob came around the desk to escort her to the front door. "I pay fifteen dollars an hour, and there are no other benefits at the moment, though we can discuss that. Is this satisfactory?"

"Yes, sir. That would be fine," Rosalie answered.

"And please do not call me Sir. My name is Jacob Hardy, and I'd appreciate it if you call me just Jacob."

"Okay, Just Jacob. I'll see you in two days." Rosalie instantly worried she'd blown it with her joke. But a glance at his face showed that her remark had only brought another small smile.

Chapter 5

Wretched reached over and punched the top of the alarm clock. He had no reason to be up, but he'd never quite figured out how to correctly set the thing.

He rolled back over and pulled the worn blanket up to his chin, wishing badly that he could return to sleep. He'd been dreaming of a warm and cheerful room, where a woman who smelled like cookies was hugging him.

Wretched knew that wishing he could return to the dream and the woman was useless. He was too awake. He sat up, stretched, and reached down to the foot of his bed to take a small cat in his arms. He hugged the soft, furry body close to his chest. "Time to get up, Tiger. Thank you for keeping me safe last night from the creatures."

The little boy went into the bathroom and splashed water on his face, drying it with the hem of his t-shirt. He ran a worn toothbrush over his teeth. He had no toothpaste, but he was grateful for a toilet that worked, a sink with running water, and the fact that after six months, Mr. Sir trusted him enough to leave the bedroom door unlocked.

Mr. Sir now called Wretched "an employee" and had explained about working for wages. An "employee" needed his own room with water to wash his body and to drink. An "employee" could leave, because he'd always come back when Mr. Sir, the "boss," had a job.

Wretched straightened out his bedclothes as best he could. He folded the extra blanket Mr. Sir had given him last week to make a cushion where Tiger would spend a good part of his day. For now, the kitty was off to explore the building and find a breakfast of bugs or mice.

Wretched turned away from his task, stretched again, and peered out the window. It was a golden day; not even the glass of the grimy window could keep out the sun's rays. Wretched loved the sun. It meant he could leave the building and do what he wanted, instead of staying in this little room. He hated it when the sun began to descend and the shadows grew, because it meant the night was coming. If the sun had been out during the day, the boy had to work for Mr. Sir that night.

But that was many hours away. For now, sunshine meant adventure, and today he would tackle his favorite place, the shopping mall. Once Wretched left the neighborhood of old abandoned buildings and entered the parking lots that eventually led to the mall, he became a different boy—a boy who could be whoever he wanted.

Inside the giant, cool structure, Wretched would sit on a bench and watch people pass by, making up stories for them and often putting himself into these stories. He would stroll the long halls, losing himself in the crowds and his own fantasies. He had become very good at this game, imaging himself as the son of a mother or father shopping in a nearby store, probably for a surprise present for him, their precious little boy.

Wretched no longer remembered if he'd actually been someone's son. Mr. Sir, who fed him and provided a safe place to sleep, and Tiger, who gave him comfort and affection, were his only family. Sometimes he longed for more food, but he'd gotten used to the feeling of hunger and accepted it. He knew he could not gain weight because if he got fat, he couldn't do his job, and without the job, there would be no Mr. Sir or Tiger. Without Mr. Sir, he wouldn't have protection from people who were bigger than him or from policemen who would lock him up.

The boy opened the cupboard above his bed and pulled out a cereal box. There was almost enough to fill the bowl, and there were no longer any bugs. He had mentioned the bugs to Mr. Sir, trying to keep the tears out of his eyes because Mr. Sir usually got angry when Wretched complained. But Mr. Sir had smiled and promised to put the cereal fresh in the box each day, beside a jar of powdered milk.

"Wait," Wretched said, pointing a finger at the returned pet, which was now purring against Wretched's legs. "We only have one bowl. I'll share my milk when I'm done."

The cat cocked his furry head as if he understood the boy's words and planted his small furry rump at Wretched's feet.

Wretched ate his cereal and then set the bowl on the floor in front of the cat. Tiger's pink tongue went to work, enjoying each lap of the treat. Wretched put the box and jar back in the cupboard so Mr. Sir could fill them again for the next meal. When the cat was done, Wretched rinsed out his bowl and spoon and put them away in the cupboard next to the cereal.

He crept down the back stairway, careful to make no sound. He had learned to be quiet most mornings because there were often strangers sleeping on the first floor—using the abandoned building as a haven from the streets. Once outside, Wretched lifted his face to drink in the warmth of the sun. He knew it would be a good day as long as he was back by dark. Until the sun fell, he had many precious hours to fill however he wanted. There would be time for work when night came and his job for Mr. Sir began.

Chapter 6

"I'd say you are pretty well locked up," Sam said as he returned to Jacob's library. Sam had been through every room in the house, checking windows and doors, while Jacob remained at his desk, talking into a tape recorder.

The author motioned for the detective to sit down, and the two faced each other across the desk.

"I can see why you're upset," Sam said. "The statues are beautiful, Mr. Hardy."

"Please, call me Jacob. They are more than just show pieces to me, and I really miss those that have disappeared. I started collecting them over five years ago. I had the lighting in the display room set up just to emphasize their perfect lines." Jacob's look was far away, and he was wringing his hands.

"And call me Sam, please," Sam said. He rubbed his chin. "I really don't understand how someone is getting in without you hearing them. You have bolts on the doors, and the windows are locked. I checked the locks to see if there was tampering, but I spotted nothing. I think you might put a better lock or a bolt on the cellar door, but there's no sign that it has been messed with."

"I suppose he or she could have somehow made a set of keys, but I'm the only one who has access to a set," Jacob said. He was studying his hands, a frown on his face.

"The one I lost last night was one of my favorites, Sam. But I didn't find a thing out of place this morning, except the missing statue. I'm a fairly light sleeper. I heard nothing—absolutely nothing at all."

Jacob stood and came around the desk, motioning for Sam to join him. The two men sat in matching armchairs before a fireplace, and Jacob poured coffee from a carafe resting on a small table between the seats. They sat in silence for a few minutes, sipping quietly and lost in their own thoughts. They looked at each other and sighed in unison, the puzzle reflected on their wrinkled brows.

"Any ideas, Sam?" Jacob finally asked.

"None at the moment," Sam replied. "But give me time. I need to talk to the few people who are around here on a regular basis, check with police to see if the department has found out anything, maybe talk to the guy you buy the statues from. Did you write out that list of people who've seen the pieces or anyone with a grudge against you?"

Jacob shook his head, a frown reappearing on his face. "Mrs. Wells is the only one who has seen the statues, other than Mr. Sterling, the man I purchased them from, and Malcolm, my agent."

"How about a secretary?" Sam asked. "You mentioned hiring one yesterday. Did you have one before? Or maybe your gardener. Has he been inside?"

"The woman I hired yesterday is the first administrative assistant I've had. My gardener has only been in my house when invited and only in the front rooms. He's never seen the statues."

Jacob looked up at Sam as if he'd just remembered something.

"I suppose I should consider Kevin Wells, Mrs. Well's husband. He was released from prison about a month before the statues started disappearing, though he wasn't there for theft. But I hate to think he might be behind this. He was proven innocent of the crime he was jailed for, and I just can't see him committing a crime that might get him back in prison. And if he were behind this, it would have to be in cahoots with Mrs. Wells. Like I said, I let Mrs. Wells in at designated times. She doesn't have her own keys."

"Where does the couple live?" Sam pulled a pen from his sports coat pocket and opened his notebook, preparing to write down an address.

"My dad built a small cottage home for them many years ago, right on the edge of this property. I value my privacy too much to have live-in servants."

Sam closed his notebook, and then rose to leave. He was pretty sure he'd found out what he could for the moment. He shook hands with Jacob. "Well, keep thinking of possibilities. I'll talk to a few people. In the meantime, have you considered locking up the statues in a cabinet or safe, so no one can get to them?"

"No," Jacob answered, anger creeping into his voice. "I want to be able to look at those pieces when

I need them. I couldn't bear to lock them away. Just studying their beauty and feeling their texture gives me great comfort and inspiration for my writing. I know you don't understand, but I won't hold them prisoner—they are the only things in this house that I truly value."

***

After the detective left, Jacob went to his trophy room and sat staring at his treasures. He picked up one of the statues and ran his hand slowly over it. *So smooth. So beautiful. So perfect.* He closed his eyes and tried to recapture the sense of calm he always felt when he rubbed the statues. Today he felt nothing but loneliness. They were, after all, only figurines. He set the statue carefully back on the shelf and left the room. His shoulders sagged slightly as he closed the door. *Maybe they wouldn't mind being locked up for a while*, he thought. But he knew he couldn't do it.

Chapter 7

Rosalie appeared at Jacob's door promptly at nine on Wednesday morning. With only a polite, "Good morning, Miz McGovern—Rosalie," he ushered her into a large library and gestured to a small desk and chair. He gave her a tape and indicated where the power button for the Dictaphone was. Within five minutes, she was alone in the big room. Rosalie picked up the manual beside the tape machine and began reading. Ten minutes later, she was sitting at the desk behind an ancient-looking typewriter, earphones on her head, and fingers flying on the keys—clack, clack, clack—a staccato beat to accompany the storytelling voice on the earphones.

Jacob had gone into his study, which adjoined the library, and shut the door between the two rooms. He sat down behind his beloved cherry desk and reached for his tape recorder. As the clicking began, his head came up and his thoughts turned to the woman in the other room. He'd noticed as they walked down the hall that she wore a light blue dress, instead of the dreary black she'd worn for the interview. A scent of honeysuckle hovered around her.

She looks so much better in that color. And the dress shows off her curves.

Jacob shook his head to clear the bizarre thought. He pushed the "record" button and picked up the microphone. He had much work to do recomposing a scene he lost during the brief attempt at using the computer. It was the pinnacle of his current book, and he'd been putting off finishing the scene, skipping ahead to the later, easier chapters. But today he was determined to rewrite what he'd lost.

Jacob dictated softly into the recorder, referring often to his handwritten notes and raising his head every once in a while when the clacking in the next room disturbed his thought processes. As the morning progressed, the noise of the typewriter began to annoy him. He wanted his quiet. He needed his quiet. After an hour and a half, he stood up, dropping his microphone on the desk.

"I can't live with this," he finally said out loud. His voice echoed against the walls of his study.

Jacob came around the desk, went to his coffee machine, poured a cup and stood awhile, sipping the hot liquid.

"It's absolutely necessary for me to concentrate if I'm going to get my book done on time," he said to the echoing walls. He realized he was talking to himself, went back to his desk, switched on the recorder and began again.

"Jacqueline's amber eyes flashed with rage at Roberto's abandonment. She stood breathing in shallow gulps, her lustrous hair almost as wild as her emotions, her breasts straining against the tight bust line of her dress. How could Roberto have betrayed her so deeply?"

Clackity clack. Tap. Tap. Tap.

"Her hand rose slowly as if it were powered by its own energy source…"

Clack clack. Clackity clack.

"…and before she could help herself, she slapped him across the face."

Clack. Clack. Tap. Tap. Tap.

Jacob stood abruptly. "I can't allow this noise," he exclaimed, his teeth clenched. "I have to have quiet."

He breathed slowly in, then out. It didn't seem to help. This time, when he came around the desk, he walked to a nearby bookshelf and picked up the picture of an older man. He gazed at the image, trying to wipe out memories of this man, his father, screaming at his mother, the maids, Jacob's caregivers, the lawyers, and business associates.

Clackity clackity clack.

Jacob slammed the picture face down on the shelf and turned away. "I will not let him win," he said softly. After a few more calming breaths, he walked to the door that joined his office with the library. It creaked slightly when he opened it.

Raising his voice he declared, "I'm sorry. You will have to go."

Rosalie's head was bent over the typewriter, a smile on her face, the earphones muffling the sound of Jacob's voice. She was so intent on finishing her paragraph; she didn't stop right away, though she'd heard the muffled command.

"You have to go," Jacob repeated with even more volume.

Her fingers stopped and the smile on Rosalie's face died as Jacob's presence and his words sank in. She took the headset off her ears and let them sit, encircling her neck.

"What did you say?"

"I'm sorry. You have to go."

"Go?" she repeated, a look of confusion on her face. "Go where?"

"Home," he said. "I can't stand the noise."

"Noise?" Rosalie said, not yet comprehending.

"Of the typewriter. The typewriter noise, it's getting in the way of my writing." Jacob felt the beginnings of a flush creep up his neck. The innocent, sparkling green eyes before him were making him feel like a louse.

"I appreciate the fact you came in today. The dress is lovely. But you have to go home now. I have to think." The flush reached his face and burned as he realized he'd just mentioned her dress.

Rosalie shook her head to clear it. It didn't seem to help. She stood slowly, but didn't move, as if trapped in her confusion.

"I'm sorry," Jacob repeated his face now quite red. *Good Lord. Why did Malcolm get me into this mess? And where had that comment about the dress come from?* He never expressed opinions about the way someone dressed.

"Why do I have to go home?" Rosalie managed to squeak out. "I've only been here a couple of hours. You haven't even looked at my typing, or said anything to me about noise. How can you just send me home?"

Joseph looked away from her, took a deep breath, and then let the air out of his lungs. He felt the color of his embarrassment begin to fade.

With his gaze focused on a row of books above Rosalie's head, he explained. "You're in the very next room from me, and I can't think with all the clatter the typewriter makes. Getting a typist was not my decision. It was my agent's idea. But I have to be able to think to write. I can't think. I need quiet. This won't work. You have to go home. I'm sorry."

Rosalie pushed her chair back from the typewriter, carefully put the cover back on the machine, turned off the Dictaphone, and stood. She walked to the chair where she'd draped her coat and picked it up. All of her movements were wooden and stiff. His eyes followed her, and he was already regretting his impulsiveness.

Is she angry at me, upset at losing the job, or reacting to that inappropriate comment about her dress?

Rosalie walked toward the library's main entrance and into the hall without a word, Jacob trailing her. She stopped when she got to the grand staircase at the front door and rested one hand on the banister to steady her trembling.

Rosalie looked up at the stairs briefly, and then turned to Jacob, her face calm.

"You have a second floor, don't you?" she asked. "In fact, you have a third floor."

"Of course," Jacob replied. It was his turn to look confused.

"Then, why don't you move me up there? I'll shut the door and you'll never know I'm here. I will tiptoe when I pass by your office. I'll bring my own coffee, so I won't need to use the kitchen. The only time you'll even hear me is when I ring the door to be let in and when I slam the door on my way out. You wanted this typing done. Your agent wanted this typing done. So what's the problem with working on another floor?"

Jacob hadn't even thought of that possibility. He was too busy trying to quell his annoyance. But he also knew her very presence in the house was disturbing him. It wasn't what he was used to—she wasn't what he was used to. He knew on some level this had little to do with her and everything to do with his own difficult personality.

After several moments of silence, he began to rub the side of his face with one hand.

"I hadn't thought of that. It will probably work. I'll have someone come in and make one of the upstairs rooms into an office. Come back next Monday, and we'll try it again."

He dropped his hand to his side, turned to Rosalie, smiled shyly and added, "We'll try it again—if you're willing, that is."

Rosalie answered with a broad grin, and Jacob

felt the lights in the hallway brighten. “See you Monday then, Just Jacob.”

Chapter 8

The minute he opened the front door of his home, Sam missed Buddy, who had always greeted him with enthusiastic licking. For Buddy, the door opening and Sam's face appearing meant it was time for the most important of daily events: the walk.

On a whim, Sam decided that even without the companionship of his beloved canine friend, there was no reason to cease the walking. Sam knew he'd enjoy the cold, refreshing air, even if it reminded him of the hole in his heart left by the death of a beloved pet, as well as the bigger hole—the loss of his family.

Sam was not as spry as he was in his years on the force, but he had no trouble tackling the three-mile route he and Buddy had taken on a regular basis. In his earlier years, Sam ran marathons—he had once traveled to D.C. to compete in the twenty-six mile U.S. Marine Marathon. As with many aspects of his life, his son's kidnapping had erased his enjoyment of competing in races. For several years after the kidnapping Sam couldn't really see the point of anything, except trying to find his son. The only distractions from the pain were putting together any clues he could find about his son and working on cases at work. They were puzzles with missing pieces; trying to figure them out kept his brain buzzing. Even though the grieving and the pain had lessened over the years, he still needed the puzzles to keep his brain sharp.

The current case was certainly not the most challenging of Sam's career, but he found it fascinating. Sam couldn't understand why a reclusive, famous author cared so much about the statues, though pride and anger over the intrusion may have played roles. Sam also had no clue why anyone would take them—it seemed a lot of risk for a little money. Together, the collection might have netted a nice chunk of money, but each piece was only worth tens of thousands of dollars, depending on the piece. And then there was the matter of how the thief accomplished the feat right under the author's nose.

After his walk, Sam strolled through the front door of his home and into his downstairs office.

"Anything new, Casey?" he asked his sunny assistant.

"You have an appointment this afternoon with Malcolm Sherburne, Jacob Hardy's agent. Here's the address. He said to show up about two. He sounds very… friendly."

"He's an agent. He better know how to sound friendly," Sam joked. "There are several more people I want to interview, Casey. I need some background info on them. See what you can find out about Kevin and Catherine Wells, Jacob's housekeeper and her husband. I also need any info on Gregory Sterling of Sterling and Company, Jacob's source for the statues, and on Horace Montgomery, the groundskeeper at Jacob's home."

Sam was sorting through his mail as he walked

into his office. He turned back to add, "I also need to know more about Jacob Hardy and his family. Jacob seems very intelligent. There must be a reason he's so isolated from society. Check with Lieutenant McCoy and Officer Danny, that handsome husband of yours, at police headquarters. They may have heard something about the family or know some of these other players."

"Do you want me to set up formal interviews with these people?" Casey asked as she made out her "to do" list for that day.

"I think I'll just catch the Wells couple at home. They live on the Hardy property. And while I'm there, I'll talk to Horace Montgomery, if I can catch him on the grounds. See what you can find out about the others, especially Kevin Wells. He was recently released from prison, so dig up some news stories and information on the crime he was convicted for. According to Jacob, he was found innocent after the fact. It may be connected in some way to these thefts."

"Now, I'm shutting myself in my office to start my file on the case."

***

Sitting down behind his desk, Sam withdrew a pile of small white cards from his desk drawer. On them, he printed the names of each person in Jacob Hardy's life and the few details he'd found out so far. The listing didn't take long—the investigation had just begun. Sighing deeply, Sam leaned back in his chair, resting his hands on his desk blotter and closed his tired eyes for a moment. He hadn't slept well the night before, and it had caught up with him. His head bobbed forward.

Jacob Hardy was caught in a web and couldn't find his way out, getting more and more entangled the harder he struggled. Suddenly, a woman appeared and spoke softly to Jacob. Sam couldn't hear the words, or see her clearly. He could only see her soothing green eyes. Whatever she was saying made Jacob stop struggling, and pieces of the web fell off to the side.

"Strange," Sam muttered as he jerked awake from the short dream.

The images of the dream were not what had bothered him. It was the memory they triggered. Sam had a similar recurring dream about himself. In it, he was immersed in quicksand and sinking, until he heard the comforting voice of a woman. It wasn't the same woman as the one in Sam's dream about Jacob and the web—this woman had eyes that were an unusual violet. But it left the same feeling of comfort.

The dream always baffled the detective. Whoever his savior was, she was not connected in any way to Barbara, Sam's wife for more than a decade and the mother of Sam's son. Barbara certainly didn't have violet eyes, and she had never been a comforting woman. In fact, when the young Sam met Barbara, part of her appeal was that she was wild, the complete opposite of Sam's religious and cold mother. Unfortunately, the wildness had taken Barbara down a path that led away from Sam. Barbara worshipped at the church of money and pursued her own agenda, which included nights on the town and other men;

Sam had found out eventually. The only thing they really had in common was Davie. Sam gave Barbara credit for loving the boy as much as he had. But her love for their son had turned to hate and blame for Sam when Davie disappeared. In the divorce proceedings, she had hurt Sam as deeply as she could.

A quiet knock at Sam's office door interrupted his reverie. Casey rolled into the office, smiled, and announced, "I have the details on Kevin Wells, if you have time."

Chapter 9

Malcolm Sherburne's width was more noticeable than his height. The five-foot-three-inch bald man didn't look obese, just evenly rounded with a jolly face, bolstered by an abundance of teeth. Leaning on a cane with his left hand, Malcolm opened the door with his right and extended it to Sam. The agent's bright, brown eyes were full of mischief, and his easy manner counterbalanced the uneasiness some people felt when they realized Malcolm couldn't quite stand upright.

"You must be Sam Osborne," he said. "I can't tell you how delighted I am to see you. I've been telling Jacob he should hire someone to clear up this theft. He's so upset about those statues. I'm afraid it's holding up his productivity."

Malcolm ushered Sam down a long hallway to an office. As he walked, Sam noticed paintings on the wall that looked like original oils, and peeking into a nearby living room as he passed, he saw an impressively furnished living room with an ornate sofa. Inside Malcolm's office, the agent pointed to a chair. He then rounded a massive, neatly ordered, and expensive-looking desk to plop in his own chair, putting his cane to the side.

"Personally, I can't see what Jacob sees in those statues," the agent continued. "They're striking, and I've heard they are worth every pretty penny

Jacob paid for them. But they're not very colorful or elaborate. To each his own, I guess," he added with a chuckle.

"When did Mr. Hardy first tell you about the statues?" Sam asked, opening his notebook.

"Right after he got the first one," Malcolm replied. "Said he was passing by the shop where he buys them, saw one in the window, and its perfection wowed him. I think the collector only had a couple at the time. Now, that collector actively hunts for them from around the world. Every time a book is published, Jacob buys another and shows it off to me. Then he just sets it up in that grand display of his, takes an afternoon off to stare at it, and gets right back to work. I believe he had twelve before they started disappearing. He puts out two to three books a year and it's been about five years."

Malcolm tilted his head to one side, and then the other, his face suddenly sobering.

"It's kind of weird, if you ask me. I'm afraid he believes they hold some magical lucky power. He's been dragging his feet on this current book, and I believe it has something to do with the thefts. I know the figurines are important to him, and if they are important to a client, they're important to me."

Sam nodded his head slowly. "It's hard to figure out how they could be taken with his house locked up so tight." His eyes found Malcolm's face, so he could see the agent's reaction to his next words. "Do you have any idea who could be behind this or why?"

"Not a clue." Malcolm's merry expression was restored. "But I like my client happy, so if you can do anything, we'd both be very grateful."

Sam studied Malcolm as the agent leaned back and rested his folded hands on his ample belly. Sam couldn't help comparing the man sitting across from him to a department-store Santa Claus, though the jolliness was already starting to wear thin. It was somehow out of proportion.

As if he could sense Sam's thoughts, Malcolm's hands came off his belly and he sat up straighter.

Sam cleared his throat. "So, Mr. Sherburne, your assessment of the statues is that they act as calming therapy for Jacob or maybe a good luck token? You think that's why they're important to him? Do you think someone is trying to disrupt his writing?"

Malcolm picked up a pencil from the desk and wove it through his fingers, then tapped one end on the desk as he thought about his answer.

"I doubt that. Not many people even know the author lives here in town. But, I believe, 'yes' on the calming effect. Sometimes I feel like Jacob is still a boy inside, and the statues are some kind of security blanket. I've known Jacob since he was a youngster, and he did have a very unhappy childhood, Sam. The statues seem to be his reward to himself, a measuring stick of his success."

Malcolm sighed heavily and leaned back again in his chair.

"Unhappy childhood?" Sam prompted.

Malcolm knitted his fingers together again, but this time laid them gently on the desk in front of him.

"You have to understand, Sam, that Jacob's father had an explosive temper. He was well known in the community as a bully. As a father, he demanded things be done a certain way, then was never satisfied with the results. I think Jacob tries to rein in his own emotions as a result.

"Mrs. Hardy, on the other hand, was a pretty useless parent. She was bedridden and always sick, or at least that's how the story goes. I spent some time in the home when Jacob first started writing, and I rarely saw his mother. She may have loved Jacob in her own way, but she gave up really early on trying to serve as a buffer between the boy and his father."

Malcolm paused to let his words sink in and to think about what he should share next. Sam knew enough to keep silent. Malcolm was doing fine on his own, spewing Hardy family secrets.

"Growing up with Mr. and Mrs. Hardy as parents, Jacob learned that it was better to never express his feelings. It's pretty interesting given the content of his books."

As he mentioned the books, the agent's face lit up. Santa Claus had returned. "Have you read the books?"

"No, not yet, but I will," Sam said. "What are the books like?"

"Amazing—given his background," Malcolm said. "Lots of romance and plenty of steamy scenes. Women just seem to gobble them up—and quite a few men too, I suspect, though I bet they don't always admit it." Malcolm winked. "My guess is they have just enough sex to keep both genders reading," he concluded.

"I'll be sure to read them," Sam commented, and then he closed his notebook. He'd gotten a feel for the agent, and his gut told him the man was not a jolly saint.

"Thanks for your time, Mr. Sherburne. I'll be sure to pick up one of his books on the way home."

"Oh, no need, Sam. Take one of my copies," Malcolm said as he turned and grabbed a book off the shelf.

"Let me know how else I can help," the agent added and then he rose and shook Sam's hand.

As Sam got into his car, he peered at the cover. A bare-chested man held a full-bosomed woman tight against his body. *She can't be able to breathe in that grasp*, Sam thought.

***

Instead of driving back to the office, Sam decided to swing by the Hardy residence and talk to the groundskeeper, Horace Montgomery. The clouds looked like they were about to spill, and Sam didn't want to miss Horace should the rain send the yard man home.

Sam spied a man in coveralls putting a power mower into a small storage shed beside the garage. "Mr. Montgomery!" Sam called out.

An unsmiling face turned towards Sam. Horace Montgomery's graying head topped a frame as tall and thin as Malcolm's had been short and wide. The man's heavily pocked face looked annoyed. Hadn't Jacob warned him that Sam might be by, and if so, why would it bother him?

"I don't want to disturb your duties, but I do have a few questions I need to ask. I'm Sam Osborne. Your employer, Mr. Hardy, hired me to look into how his statues are disappearing." Sam extended his hand, but Horace looked at it as if were an unwelcome foreign object. Still, after a moment, the gardener took off a glove, wiped his hand on his coveralls and completed the handshake.

"Don't have much time," Horace mumbled. "Goin' to rain soon. Got to get my work done before it comes."

"Just a few questions, Mr. Montgomery. I promise not to keep you."

Horace pointed to two chairs sitting under a huge oak tree, and the two men walked slowly to the spot. It was pleasant sitting under the tree; a cool breeze hinted at the rain to come, but couldn't quite push away the humidity.

"Mr. Hardy told me he didn't think you'd seen the statues," Sam began. "He said the only times you've been in the house were to discuss the grounds."

The edges of a thick mustache turned upward, but the smile never reached the gardener's eyes.

"So have you seen them?" Sam prodded.

"Well, Mr. Osborne. I hope you don't go and tell 'im, because what he don't know won't hurt him and I need this job. But yeah, I seen 'em once, and let me tell ya, I wasn't impressed."

"You found them to be lacking in some way?" Sam asked. "How did you get access to them?"

"They sure don't look like they're worth much. I seen the same sort of thing in Pier One. I guess he's got older models, but it still looks like junk to me. I don't question Mr. Hardy, though. He may be a little touched in the head, but he pays well."

Horace peered closely at Sam. "You ain't gonna tell Jacob, are you? I'm jes' trying to be honest here."

"And how is it, exactly, that you saw the statues?" Sam asked again.

Horace sat up straighter in his seat. "Well, it weren't really planned, Mr. Osborne. I believe it was last summer sometime. It was a hot day, and Mr. Hardy was meeting with his agent in town. That's why Mrs. Wells invited me in, I guess. She's a nice lady, and I think she was lonely on account of her husband bein' in jail. She offered me lemonade. I guess it was her break.

"Anyhow, we got to talking, and she told me about how obsessed Mr. Hardy is with the things. Guess I was curious, cause when she asked me kind of sly-like if I'd like to take a peek, I said, 'sure.'

"I expected to see somethin' really spectacular from what she told me. But they weren't even white or a pretty color—just kind of dirty-looking. Can't understand why anyone would pay money for them, or enjoy spending time looking at the things."

Sam hadn't taken out his notebook. He put one foot on the opposite knee, in the typical male cross-your-legs fashion, and sat back, smiling at Horace in an attempt to put the other man at ease.

"I guess we all like different things. And I am not here to get you in any trouble, Mr. Montgomery. I'm just here to get some answers. How long have you worked for Mr. Hardy?"

"Goin' on seven years now. Course it's only part-time. I work for some of the other homeowners around this area, cuttin' grass and handy man jobs usually."

"And you've only seen the statues that one time?" Sam asked.

"Yeah. Probably been in that house only half a dozen times since Jacob's daddy died and Jacob hired me on. I'd done a few odd jobs for the older Hardy. From what Catherine says, I'm damn lucky it was only odd jobs, 'cause I'm not sure I coulda stood working for him. I knew Oswald Hardy when we were in school, and I remember he was a bear even then. According to Catherine, he became a grizzly when he got older."

Sam filed that tidbit away in his brain, and

then looked at the sky, deciding he'd better cut his visit short. He rose to go, just as he realized he was too late—the rain suddenly burst from the sky. Sam was soaked by the time he reached his car. He didn't think Horace Montgomery would get any more work done that day.

Sam sat in his car and made the decision to go home instead of staying to interview Mrs. Wells. He needed to get out of his wet clothes, freshen up, and get some lunch before making the long drive to Hope, Pennsylvania, to interview Gregory Sterling, the antiques merchant who sold Jacob the statues. Sam wouldn't be home until late that evening, so he'd have to wait until then for his comfortable chair and a beer. And maybe tonight, some reading of Jacob Hardy's book would give him insight into the reclusive author.

Chapter 10

Wretched sat on his small bed with only Tiger for company. Rain pounded against the glass window. He hated the rain. It meant he had to stay inside—there would be no adventures today. On rainy days, Mr. Sir always checked in on him. The man was usually in a bad mood on rainy days, since there would be no work that night. Even so, Wretched felt glad for those visits sometimes, because he was afraid of thunderstorms, though he'd never admit it.

The building where Wretched lived was old and falling apart, and it smelled particularly bad during rainstorms. Rain came through places in the walls and ceiling, dripping steadily in a rhythm that helped Wretched nap away the hours, if there was no thunder. Today, instead of sleeping, Wretched stared dejectedly at the water drizzling down his wall as he stroked Tiger's back. He had already decided what he would do today, before the rain went and ruined it.

Wretched had decided against the mall, choosing instead his second favorite spot, the big park across from the mall. He loved to sit on a bench and watch families. He especially liked to watch the children play. Several times, one of them had approached Wretched, trying to entice him to join in a game or a race. Wretched was too shy and too afraid to do so, though. If Mr. Sir ever caught him talking to the people in the park, Wretched knew how angry his boss would be, and the boy knew better than to get Mr. Sir angry. It made the older man do things he later apologized for, like hitting Wretched and keeping his food from him. Wretched made sure Mr. Sir didn't get angry very often. Sometimes Mr. Sir was even nice. Wretched remembered last Christmas when Mr. Sir had surprised his young employee with a winter coat wrapped in Christmas paper. The coat wasn't new, but it was warm and soft, and on cold nights, it served as another blanket.

Occasionally, Wretched wondered what a different life would be like. The thought didn't last long. He rarely questioned the way he lived. He couldn't always figure out why Mr. Sir did the things he did, or asked Wretched to do certain things. But Wretched remembered enough about his past life to know he was better off with Mr. Sir. If it wasn't for Mr. Sir, Wretched knew he wouldn't survive. As long as Mr. Sir wasn't angry, the man brought food for Wretched's belly, and gave the boy clothes when he outgrew his old ones. Once in a while, Mr. Sir patted the boy's head or shoulder, and told him what a good "employee" he was.

Mr. Sir was security and the small boy only had to keep from upsetting his protector to keep that security in place. This last week, the boy hadn't been so lucky. Wretched had dropped one of the items Mr. Sir had asked him to get, and a tiny ear broke off. Wretched tried to put it back on, but he had no glue. He'd scrubbed and scrubbed the place where the ear had been, hoping to make a smooth spot where the chip was. The boy knew he had failed when he saw Mr. Sir's face. Anger crackled in the man's eyes as he slowly took off his belt. The anger was much worse in

Wretched's mind than the actual sting of the belt as it hit his back. The boy was used to pain, and he knew it would go away. His back stung only a little now, but the fear was always there. Would Mr. Sir leave and never come back? Would the bad people Mr. Sir always talked about come to get Wretched?

He shook himself, lifted Tiger, and began to stroke the kitten's back. Then he did what he always did when he needed something to take his mind off of the fear: he imagined nice things and tried to put his thoughts there. Sitting on his bed, his mind left the dirty building and went to the park across from the mall.

Wretched turned his face upwards, just as he'd done last week. The sun had greeted his face, warming the boy through and through and making him feel light and airy. And then, Wretched heard music. It drew the boy, and he rose from the bench to follow the sound. He could sense that something great and wonderful was happening near the mall that day. And sure enough, just at its edges, workers were erecting a small carnival. Wretched remembered a few other carnivals that had gone up close to the mall: the tinny notes of the carousel and other rides, the smell of the cotton candy and popcorn, the smiles on the faces of the people passing in and out of the aisles.

Wretched walked slowly towards the magic, studying the fence around the perimeter, until he found a place where his small frame could just fit through without anyone seeing him. It was early in the process of setting up the carnival; the rides were still being assembled, and the tents had not yet been raised. The music must have been coming from one of the rides that had already been built, and Wretched moved towards the sound. He spotted the giant red saucers twirling and twirling. Wretched wondered again what it would feel like to ride one of those machines. Would he be brave enough?

His thoughts were interrupted by a gravelly voice. "Want some popcorn, Son?"

Wretched turned to see a man near a booth holding out a box. He could see that the man had only a few teeth, but his face was not scary. He was smiling, and said, "It's free. I'm just testing my popper machine. See if it's okay for me, will ya"

Wretched reached for the warm treat, took a handful, and put it in his mouth. "It's wonderful," he said between chews. "Thanks, mister."

Munching on the popcorn, Wretched walked slowly through the carnival, savoring the bustling scene as well as the treat. He knew that before long, many people would crowd the fairway. Already, interested families were watching the comings and goings from outside the fence. Children were hopping up and down in excitement, begging their mothers to bring them back when the carnival opened. He couldn't help wondering what it would be like to have someone hold tight to his hand so he wouldn't get lost. Except for his occasional dream of a blond lady who smelled like cookies and held him close, Wretched had no idea what a mom or dad felt like. Still, thinking about the blond lady and the popcorn delighting his taste buds, Wretched smiled. For a moment, he was happy.

Now, back in the room where he spent many days, he remembered that happy feeling. He could still taste the salt and butter, and feel his surprise at the kindness of the man who had given him the treat. He still felt the wonder that overcame him as he'd stood on the fairway watching the activity. His reverie was broken, however, with the rattle of the doorknob. The boy was suddenly back to the present, smelling bad smells, instead of popcorn.

Chapter 11

Sam cursed as he drove the two hours to Hope; he hated driving in the rain. He was on his way to the home of art dealer Gregory Sterling. Sam's assistant Casey had set up the appointment, and Sam was not one to be late. The little umbrella he carried in his glove compartment was no match for this wind and downpour, and he was thoroughly soaked a second time that day after dashing from his car to Sterling's front door.

Sam got wetter as he rang the doorbell. At long last, the door creaked open and an elderly gentleman dressed in a butler's uniform let Sam in. The butler grimaced slightly as Sam dripped water onto the foyer floor. When Sam explained the purpose of his visit, the butler nodded politely and led the detective past a grand staircase and down a long hallway. Like in Malcolm Sherburne's home, the halls were lined with paintings, but these were displayed in heavily gilded frames that looked formal and old.

The study was aglow from a large fire in the fireplace—a welcome sight for the very wet and cold detective. Yet Sam could not shake the chill he felt and he suspected it was partly from the home itself. Its grandness—high ceilings, ornate furniture, big rooms, and scrollwork on most of the walls—didn't help, making it feel more like a museum than a home.

Sam held his hands out to the fire before sitting down in a stiff-backed chair in front of the fireplace. He allowed his eyes to roam the room's interior, studying it more closely. Every surface was highly polished and gleaming. The lamps had beaded shades. A desk with intricately carved legs rested against a far wall. Heavy marble and bronze statues accented the leather-bound books on the shelves. The room had little appeal for a man with Sam's simple tastes.

The detective's dampened disposition was not improved by the wait. By the time Gregory Sterling walked through a door at the opposite end of the room, Sam had been sitting for twenty minutes.

Sam rose to greet the art dealer, who was just over six feet tall with a lean frame, adorned in a formally cut suit that seemed to go along with the frown etched upon his face. His black eyes, set close together, bore into Sam from a face with many wrinkles and not even a hint of friendliness.

"Gregory Sterling," the man said. Gregory sat down stiffly in a chair at a ninety-degree angle from Sam's. The dealer perched on the chair's edge as if ready to get back up immediately.

"How may I help you?"

Sam tried his usual smile, but the chill in his bones kept it from feeling natural.

"As I'm sure my assistant explained I'm here on behalf of Jacob Hardy, who is looking into the disappearance of some of the statues you sold to him." Sam pulled out his notebook and noticed his host relax just a bit.

"Ah, yes. I sold Mr. Hardy twelve exquisite

statues—very valuable, very collectible." The level of enthusiasm in the dealer's voice kicked up a notch. "They were made before the Ming dynasty and are valued at about thirty thousand dollars each. Several are worth even more."

"Then, you've no doubt heard that three of the pieces were taken from his home. This week another went missing," Sam said.

Gregory Sterling's enthusiasm evaporated and his voice took on a scolding tone. "Of course I've heard. Mr. Hardy shared that information with me in hopes that I'd know something, and I spoke with someone from the police department. I told Jacob the pieces should be locked up in a secure vault, or a display case in a locked room. He obviously did not listen to my advice. It was foolish to keep such valuable pieces out in the open."

Sam's scribbling stopped as he looked at the dealer, wondering why the man would refer to a regular client's actions as "foolish."

"The house itself is locked up tight, Mr. Sterling. Even the windows are secured and Mr. Hardy is usually at home."

Gregory cleared his throat and sat back in his chair, a smug expression on his face. "I suppose he considered that sufficient, Mr. Osborne. But it didn't protect his valuable statues, did it?"

Sam resumed his writing to cover his distaste for the art dealer.

"And what does all this have to do with me,

Mr. Osborne? I sell him the pieces. I never see them after they leave my shop." After a pause, Gregory added, "He's rather an odd sort, really. Never has much to say, but he always knows exactly what he wants when he sees it, and he handles the pieces as if they hold some mystical power. He never even asks the price."

Sam made no comment. He wondered, though, why the agent made it sound more like criticism, rather than praise. The detective was sure that a few of the statues' prices went up the moment Jacob indicated interest in them.

Sam sat back and studied the man before him. Gregory Sterling looked relaxed in his chair now. He wasn't looking at Sam or Sam's notebook. He was picking imaginary pieces of lint from his suit sleeve.

"How long have you known Jacob?" Sam asked, returning to his writing.

"Since the day he was born," Gregory replied, surprising Sam enough to look up from the notebook.

"His father and I did business for many years," the dealer explained. "Oswald had a taste for fine antiques. He even bought his son a crib from the 1800s. Oswald and I kept in touch over those years, and we became quite friendly. We would have dinner once or twice a year and went on several hunting trips together."

Yes, I can see you as a "friend" to a tyrant, Sam thought. But he kept his opinion to himself.

"Is Jacob very much like his father, then?" Sam probed, just to see what the dealer would say.

"Far from it," Sterling affirmed. "Jacob was a shy, withdrawn boy. Most of his life, he was schooled at home by tutors the Hardys hired. By contrast, Oswald was full of spirit—a fine hunter and sportsman, who also had a shrewd nose for business."

Without any further prompting by Sam, Gregory continued his negative assessment of the younger Hardy.

"I always felt Jacob was a big disappointment to his father. The boy hated all sports; he wouldn't go hunting with his father and also hated fishing. He got beat up a lot in school in his younger years, which is why I think they took him out. I guess the mother insisted her son be kept safe and wouldn't even consider letting him play sports. Jacob mostly just kept to himself and read a lot. I only met him a few times when he was a youngster. Unlike with Oswald, Jacob's relationship with me is strictly business."

Sam heard a soft chuckle.

"In contrast, his father and I shared many laughs. Oswald was a big outdoorsman, loved his liquor, and liked the women, even though he was married."

Sam looked up from his notebook to see a smirk on the dealer's face.

"And did you know Jacob's mother?"

As the detective's purposeful reference to

Oswald's wife hit home, Gregory's black eyes flashed, and he sat forward slightly in his seat.

"Millie was a bit of a wet rag almost from the first and a hypochondriac. She rarely left her bedroom in later years. I always figured Oswald married her for her money—her parents were well to do. It was certainly not for her looks or her charm."

Sam had no idea why this man was spilling his guts about Jacob Hardy's parents. The information was certainly useful in understanding the author, even if it was one-sided and appalling. The detective decided, however, that it was time to get away from the gossip. He led the conversation towards the collection of statues. He wanted to know where they were sourced, what other types of customers Gregory Sterling had, and what other types of collections the dealer offered.

After about twenty minutes, Sam politely ended the interview and stood to leave. Gregory walked him to the front door, but didn't extend a hand to shake. The dealer simply opened the large door and gestured towards the outside.

This time, Sam was glad for the wet weather. He hoped the rain that fell as he made his way to his car would wash away the feeling of disgust he felt at the dealer's eagerness to share "dirt" on Jacob.

Chapter 12

At six thirty a.m. Friday, Jacob sat eating his breakfast and savoring the reality that today, like yesterday's rainy, productive day, would allow him to stick to his usual routine without interruption. The only wrinkle in his day of writing was a meeting scheduled with Sam just before lunch.

Jacob was still bothered by the fact that starting Monday, there'd be someone else in the house every day, even though that someone—Rosalie McGovern—would be upstairs most of the time. He wasn't convinced having her there was the right thing for him, and he didn't like the change in routine that was involved.

Visualizing someone else working on the tapes he was dictating also bothered the author. Writing the words down himself or talking into the machine was one thing. Having another person hear those tapes before he could finalize his work or polish those words was quite another. And what would she think about the steamy scenes? He hadn't dictated one of those scenes for this book yet, because he wasn't at a point in the story that called for it. But he wasn't sure he'd be comfortable talking them out knowing she'd be listening to him.

Feeling agitation beginning to sprout, Jacob decided he needed a few minutes with his statues. He set his breakfast dishes aside to be collected by Mrs.

Wells and rose to walk to his trophy room. There, he plopped down on the armchair where he always sat and looked at the remaining statues. The agitation grew as he looked at the four empty spaces where his precious pieces once stood.

As his agitation turned to anger, Jacob stood, picked up one of his statues and began to stroke it gently.

"You must not get angry. You must be calm. Anger is senseless and unproductive." He was chanting the words softly as he had done many times. In his mind, he saw the face of Oswald, red and screaming obscenities.

"Your father is gone. You have control. You choose to be calm."

And that calm came to him, eventually. Jacob put the statue carefully back on its shelf and left the room. In his study, he turned on the tape machine, sat back in his chair, and began to talk. Seeing his hero and heroine in his mind, he soon lost himself completely in his words.

He didn't think about what he was doing for the next two-and-a-half hours, until a small tabletop alarm went off indicating lunchtime was approaching. After that he had his meeting with the detective. He usually spent a few minutes clearing the cobwebs by visiting his statues. But Jacob remained seated, thinking how blessedly quiet the morning had been and how everything was about to change with the addition of the typist.

Jacob got up from his chair and began to pace

in front of his desk, his hand stroking his chin.

Why again, was he doing this—allowing a person in his home every day?

My damn agent wants me to work more efficiently. But do I really care?

He knew deep down that having an assistant made sense for an author who refused to use computers. He heard again the sound of the typewriter keys clicking and clicking, he pictured the empty spaces on his shelves where the missing statues had been, and then he felt his peace of mind slipping through his fingers.

Jacob stopped abruptly in front of the shelf where his father's picture glared out at him

"By God," he said to himself. "There's nothing I can do about the past—Father is dead. The statues are gone. But there is definitely something I can do about the future!"

He picked up the phone, ready to ring Rosalie and call off the whole assistant/typist deal. He did not have to put up with a stranger in his house.

However, when Rosalie answered the phone, her voice fluttery and cheerful, Jacob said nothing. He pictured the blue dress, the green eyes, her soft curves, and smelled her honeysuckle scent.

"Hello? Is someone on the line? Do you have the wrong number?"

"This is Jacob Hardy. We're a little behind on the book. Could you stay until at least six your first few days?"

"Oh, Mr. Hardy. Good to hear from you. I can stay as late as you like."

"Very well, then," he said and hung up.

He closed his eyes and shook his head. *What the hell is wrong with me?* He sighed. *I could get a lot done over the weekend.*

Jacob picked up the Dictaphone and began to talk—lunch, Sam, and the typist forgotten.

Chapter 13

The gloom of the previous day's weather gave way to a welcoming sun. The humidity was replaced by a light breeze that left the air feeling new and crisp. Sam took advantage of the pleasant weather and began his day with a brisk walk. It cleared his head of the heavy task of pouring over his notes from the day before. Like the sky, Sam's brain was fresh this morning, ready to tackle the task of getting more input on Jacob Hardy's world.

Sam was on his way to talk to Catherine and Kevin Wells. He knew from Jacob that Catherine Wells worked in the Hardy mansion two days a week, cleaning the house from top to bottom. The rest of the week she was only in the home long enough to deliver meals and food supplies. She cooked hot meals for most of Jacob's dinners, and an occasional lunch, in her own kitchen at the Wells' cottage on the Hardy grounds. She then delivered them to the main house at meal time. At the beginning of each week, Jacob and Catherine worked out a schedule of when Catherine would need access to the home—an arrangement that had gone on for many years.

Catherine had been married to Kevin for thirty-five years. She remained convinced of his innocence of the robbery for which he was accused and had been his main champion during the trial. According to Jacob, Kevin had no access to the Hardy mansion, and Catherine didn't have a set of keys—Jacob let her in and out according to the prearranged schedule. But the possibility that Catherine let Kevin in at some point had to be considered.

This morning, Sam parked at the Hardy home's main entrance but walked around the residence and down a path to the Wells' house, arriving just after ten-thirty in hopes of catching them both at home. He had made no appointment but found Catherine at home and seemingly happy to have him interrupt her day. They talked in the kitchen, so she could continue making rolls.

Catherine Wells was a sixty-year-old bundle of energy—a sturdy woman who, despite a few dozen extra pounds, moved quickly and efficiently. Her eyes sparkled full of pleasure at having someone visit.

"It's horrible that anyone would take away that dear man's beloved statues," Catherine said to Sam. She clutched a flour-covered hand to her bosom and then seemed to realize the mess she was making. She grabbed a dishtowel to dust off her hands and apron. "Personally, I can't see what he likes so much about those figurines, but they do seem to give him comfort and pleasure."

Sam knew this long-time employee of the Hardy's must be filled to the brim with information about the family, and he saw right away it wouldn't be hard to tap the source. Within a few sentences, he could tell she was one of those people who enjoyed the very act of conversing.

"How long have you known Mr. Hardy?" Sam prodded.

Catherine resumed kneading dough. "Oh, I've worked in the Hardy home for over forty years. I came here with Millie Foxe when she married Oswald Hardy." Her head came up from her task, and she turned to gaze out the window.

"Millie was such a cheerful youngster before the marriage, petite and friendly. She loved to dance and play tennis and have friends over when we lived in her parent's big house. Everyone loved her.

"Oswald Hardy seemed to be quite taken with her for about six months—the three months they dated, and the three after they got married."

She turned towards Sam, and her sparkling eyes dimmed a little. "But the minute she announced she was pregnant, he changed. He suddenly acted like he was tired of her, that she was a burden on his grand household, and that he had better things to do than lavish attention on his young bride. The more he ignored her, the more she lost her spirit."

Catherine admitted to Sam that she had never understood why the two had decided to have a child—if, indeed, a decision had been made. Neither Millie nor Oswald seemed to find joy from the pregnancy or the boy's arrival into the world.

The housekeeper put her dough in a bowl and used the dishcloth to cover it. The bowl went on top of the warming oven. Catherine turned back from the oven to give Sam her full attention.

"Oswald never did understand that child. And Millie just didn't seem to care much. I guess it made for a pretty unhappy childhood for a boy who, at least when he was young, was always trying to please them."

Catherine washed her hands at the kitchen sink, and came to sit across from Sam at the kitchen table. Her eyes took on a distant look that told Sam her mind was returning to Jacob's earlier days. Suddenly, Sam saw a spark of anger.

"I don't know why it is that some people who could really love a child can't have one—and some who have children act like they're a nuisance."

Sam wondered whether the fact she and her husband Kevin had never had children caused them grief.

He changed the subject.

"Do you know why Jacob is so taken with the statues? They're beautiful and they cost a lot of money, but he seems devastated by their loss. Does he have other possessions that mean that much to him?"

Catherine thought for a moment, her head slightly tilted, and then closed her eyes and gently shook her head.

"No. He's not at all materialistic. I don't think he even sees how grand his home is, though he keeps it up well enough."

She opened her eyes, and Sam saw an idea form behind their hazel depths.

"You know, Mr. Osborne, I believe he likes the things because they provide him company, but they're not alive. They can't judge him. I've seen him sit and talk to the statues, though I know he doesn't realize I'm there. It's almost like they are some kind of therapy. Does that make sense?"

Sam wasn't one to render an opinion on someone else's theories of the psyche. "Do you have any idea who could have done this, Mrs. Wells, or how a burglar could have gotten into the house?"

"I've thought about it a bit and looked around the house, but I'm no detective. I do not understand how this could be happening right under his nose." Catherine got up and took off her apron, opened the refrigerator, and peered down at the watch on her wrist.

Sam used the time to study the warm kitchen. It was still cluttered from Catherine's roll-making, but filled with shiny clean pots and pans hanging from hooks, a big fern plant in a corner, a row of hooks for aprons, measuring cups, and oversized spoons hanging from straps. The room felt friendly and comfortable.

"Is your husband at home?" Sam asked.

"I think he's just coming down the path," she said, glancing out her window. She held a covered dish she'd taken out of the refrigerator. "You're welcome to sit and wait for him here. I need to take Jacob's lunch up to the house, though I don't know how much he'll eat. He seems nervous these last two days. I think having a typist coming in has him spooked. He keeps muttering about changes in the schedule that will need to be made." She wore a bemused expression on her face though, as if she thought the changes might do the recluse some good.

Without another word, Catherine Wells scurried out the door, off toward the main house.

***

Through the window, Sam saw a man he assumed was Kevin Wells stop to kiss his wife on the cheek. The two said nothing to each other. When Kevin entered the house, he started at seeing a stranger sitting at his kitchen table, sipping tea.

"I'm Sam Osborne," Sam said. "I'm the detective Mr. Hardy hired to find out who is stealing his statues."

Kevin Wells seemed agitated and stood awkwardly in his own kitchen, as if he were unsure how to react to Sam's announcement. Catherine's husband sported a full head of snowy white hair and bushy eyebrows that stretched almost without interruption across his forehead. He was about half as wide as his wife, and Sam noted Kevin's limp as he walked down the lane.

"I suppose you think I stole those damn statues," Kevin said defiantly before Sam could even formulate a question. "Well, I didn't—but the facts don't seem to make much difference with you cops. I was in prison, so I'm automatically the number one suspect, even though I committed no crime. "

Sam shook his head and gestured to a chair, hoping Kevin Wells would sit. "I'm not accusing anyone of anything, and I'm not a cop. I'm a private investigator," he said calmly. "I'm just questioning anyone who might have access to the house. Since you're married to Catherine, I assume you could get into the house if you wanted. Isn't that so?"

"Well, sure I can, and I have gone into the house a few times these past months to talk to my wife or to deliver her meals," he said with a sharp tone. He sat down and added, "Mr. Osborne, Catherine showed me those statues once. Just once. To tell you the truth, I thought they were pretty pitiful looking things. I know they are worth something to Jacob Hardy, but they're nothing to me. And I sure ain't going to steal something the first night I get out of the damn joint, which is when that first one disappeared. How stupid do you think I am?" He sat back in his chair and glared at Sam.

Sam sat back in his own chair and pushed his teacup away from him. "As I said before, Mr. Wells, I am not accusing anyone at this point—I'm just trying to gather information about possibilities. I know that DNA evidence cleared you of the robbery. I am not here about that crime—it's in your past. But since you have been in that house, do you have any ideas how one could get into a completely locked up home like that? Have you ever seen anyone suspicious hanging around the property?"

"No," Wells said, his voice still agitated. "I seen no one, and I ain't got nothing to do with those damn statues!"

"I hear you, Mr. Wells. And I am sure you can account for your late evening hours since you were released. Most of the statues were taken during the night, or so I've surmised since Jacob is at home most of the time."

"My wife and I go to bed around ten every

night, and it doesn't take me but a minute before I am snoring happily—all night long. Catherine is my alibi. "

"Understood," Sam said simply then stood to leave. He would be back to talk to Kevin, but it was close to eleven-thirty, and the detective had agreed to meet Jacob at the main house. At the kitchen door, Sam turned back and added, "Thanks to you and Catherine for your time, Mr. Wells. I'm headed up to Jacob's to look around again. I'll be in touch."

On the path, Sam breathed in a cleansing breath. He was glad to leave Kevin Wells and his hostility behind, yet he couldn't really blame the man for not wanting to be interviewed about a robbery so soon after spending time in jail. Sam found it difficult, however, to put Kevin Wells' negativity and hostility together with a woman as cheerful and full of life as Catherine Wells. Maybe Kevin had been a different kind of man before prison.

Chapter 14

After Jacob's call, Rosalie stared at the phone for five minutes thinking, *What have I gotten myself into?* There was something about Jacob's hesitancy that made Rosalie wonder what intentions had been in asking her to stay late.

What is it about me that disturbs him so much? Is it just the fact I'm female? Is he really that anti-social?

She knew the man was a recluse, but she had to wonder why. He was attractive despite his uptight, outdated look. His face was all angles and sharpness, almost aristocratic in appearance. His chestnut brown hair curled just slightly. He towered over her in height, and his clothes were too formal – stiff suit pants and dry-cleaned, button-down shirts. The man probably didn't own a pair of blue jeans or khakis, yet the stiff clothes didn't detract from his handsomeness. *Why does this man live all alone?*

And where did his words come from? Rosalie had read just enough in her furious few hours of typing to know his current book matched his others—he had a way with words that made reading a leisurely pleasure. She also knew his novels had the reputation of being particularly sexy, though she hadn't come across that in the few chapters she'd typed.

"Rosalie!" Doris called from the bottom of the stairs, snapping Rosalie out of her reverie.

"I'm coming," Rosalie called back as she stood. She glanced briefly in the mirror and for once, wasn't unhappy with the green eyes, shiny hair, and curvy body reflected there.

***

"I've made a delicious beef roast for our lunch today," Doris said as Rosalie settled at the table. The older woman placed steaming platters of beef, potatoes, and corn on the table, enough for at least four people. "You can have leftovers for dinner tonight while I'm away at the Friday night prayer meeting." Doris stopped her ministrations long enough to look up at Rosalie, a gleam in her eye. "It must be very exciting to work for an author. What kind of books does he write?"

Rosalie didn't know how to answer. She didn't think her mother would approve of the kind of steamy romance for which this particular author was famous. She was suddenly glad her mother wasn't a reader.

"I'm not too familiar with his work yet. I think they're some kind of romance," she fibbed.

Doris sat down with a dreamy look on her face. She tilted her head.

"He must be debonair and sophisticated. Maybe a poet at heart. And all that money!" Her gaze found its way back to Rosalie's face.

“Is he handsome as well as wealthy, dear? I’ve heard he has a lot of money.” Her words were followed by a scowl. “He didn’t try any funny business with you, did he?”

“Mother! Of course not. He’s a professional. A very quiet guy. He kind of keeps to himself, actually.” Rosalie began cutting the tender beef. “And yes, he’s quite good-looking.”

“I knew it! I remember his father from school,” Doris interrupted. “He was the star quarterback and always had the girls drooling over him.”

Doris served herself a good portion of the beef before she added, “Although, I can’t say that I thought much of Oswald. He was very much a bully—rude and very crude. I don’t think his parents were very good Christians.”

Doris didn’t see her daughter’s eyes roll. Rosalie was curious to know more.

“What was his mother like?” she asked in a soft voice.

“Oh, Millie Hardy was nice enough, given her very rich daddy. She wasn’t stuck-up at all. Kind of delicate, as I remember, with sort of a horsey face.”

Doris picked up the potato bowl, served herself a heaping helping, and then handed the bowl to Rosalie, who set it down without taking any.

“We were all surprised when the two of them started dating. Aren’t you eating your potatoes? I cooked them just for you!”

Rosalie, who had been gazing over her mother's shoulder and out the living room window with her thoughts partially on Oswald Hardy and partially on his son, brought her attention back to the table and took a small spoonful of the spuds.

"Rosalie. That's not enough to fill you up!" Doris said. She reached across the small table, picked up the bowl, took the spoon from Rosalie's grasp, and then piled more on her daughter's plate.

Rosalie sighed deeply, but resolved not to eat much. She wasn't really hungry, and she really wanted to lose weight. To distract her mother, Rosalie asked what the older woman had planned for the rest of the day.

The next thirty minutes were an outpouring of mundane details about the planning of a church bazaar, but Rosalie was content. She knew that with a few simple nods of her head she could half listen and leave the rest of her brain to think about the author, his enormous house, his strange behavior, and his books.

***

That night, in her too-frilly bed, in the too-frilly room her mother had "surprised" her with, Rosalie was still thinking about the author and her new job. If she could keep this one for a while, she'd have enough to join one of those diet plans, a gym, or buy some nice clothes, or maybe even plan another trip away to someplace exotic. Meanwhile, she had a job that was interesting and involved reading.

Wouldn't it be nice to have someone to share the

excitement of traveling, or the plots of books with, she thought as she lay wide-awake. *Maybe I should try getting into the dating scene again.* The thought made her sigh deeply and turn over to punch her pillow.

Who am I kidding? I'll never find someone who likes me. I'm too outspoken and I refuse to play the meek game just to get along with a male for the night.

Then Rosalie remembered what lunch had been like earlier that day with her own mother. Rosalie often let Doris ramble while her thoughts drifted to the plot of the most recent novel she was reading, or a story in the paper, or something she had seen on the news.

Rosalie turned onto her back and stared at the ceiling.

Maybe I can use the same method to flatter a guy into thinking I'm hanging on his every word.

She laughed out loud.

What would be the point in that? Rosalie thought. She turned over onto her side and went to sleep.

Chapter 15

The following Wednesday, Jacob was seated at his dining room table, preparing to eat the lunch he fixed for himself at least once a week—a sandwich made from egg salad that Mrs. Wells left in the refrigerator, an apple or pear cut in quarters, a pickle, and a glass of milk. His napkin was unfolded and lying in his lap. His eyes were on his plate. His mind was fixated on what he had written that morning. He was reaching for his sandwich when a soft rustle interrupted his thoughts. The author looked up to find Rosalie standing at the other end of the long table, a paper bag in hand. She smiled shyly. "It is so nice outside that I thought I might eat my lunch in the yard, if that's okay with you?"

Jacob knew he was glaring at her, but he couldn't seem to help it. No one ever interrupted his lunch. He wasn't sure why it irritated him.

In response to his silence, Rosalie nervously added, "I was going to sit under that big oak tree. You have such a beautiful yard."

Still, he said nothing. Just sat there holding the sandwich halfway to his mouth.

Rosalie finally turned around and started towards the doorway, sighing heavily. The minute she turned away, words came out of Jacob's mouth that surprised both of them, "You can join me here at the table, if you wish."

Where did that come from? Jacob wondered. *The woman will no doubt prattle.*

"Thank you," she said softly. "I didn't mean to disturb your quiet time."

"Please, sit down," Jacob said, his tone now polite. But he already felt peculiar and out of sorts; he could feel his temperature rising and his heart's pace quickening.

Rosalie slid into the chair at the foot of the long table. Her heartbeat picked up speed, and she calmed herself by opening her paper bag and taking out half her sandwich. She would bury the other half in the trash, somewhere her mother wouldn't see. Next, Rosalie took out a paper towel, unfolded it and put in on her lap. Finally, she unscrewed the top of a plastic container that held fresh peaches, which she herself had added to her lunch bag this morning. Feeling his eyes on her, however, she looked up and repeated, "Thank you."

Neither of them knew how to handle the silence that followed. Jacob sat, not eating his lunch. He looked around the room, trying to come up with some topic of conversation. Rosalie took out a spoon and laid it next to the peach container. Clearing her throat she managed to squeak out, "This is very nice of you. It's a lovely dining room table… and big."

Jacob actually smiled at her comment, and Rosalie was amazed at the transformation. He was handsome without a smile, but he was striking and appealing when his lips turned upwards.

"I feel like you're in another room," he said, his voice echoing against the walls. "Why don't you move down here beside me?"

Rosalie looked around her as if trying to locate who had issued the invitation. She picked up her sack, her sandwich, her container and her spoon and carried it all to his end of the table. She sat down caddy-corner from him.

"This is nice," she said, rearranging her lunch in its new location. But she was already nervous about what she could say next.

Jacob broke the silence this time. "How is the typing going?" Rosalie had been at it for three days now.

"Oh, fine," she replied enthusiastically, glad to have a direction for the conversation. "The room I'm using is set up very nicely and comfortably. I do love this house, or at least what I've seen of it. I spotted the laptop on the shelf and even powered it up."

She took a small bite of her sandwich and carefully chewed it before continuing. "My friends insist it's a much easier way to save written material, so I might try to figure it out. But I much prefer the typewriter. I hope that's okay for now."

"Of course it is. My agent insisted I get the dratted computer to try to compose at the keyboard. Use the machine if you want, but I'm getting along pretty well with my notes and my tape machine. The computer has a mind of its own, and my very heavy fingers do not get along with its thinking."

"Oh, I know what you mean!" Rosalie said. "I get my rhythm going strong, then look up to see my fingers were on the wrong letters. It's pretty incredible what gibberish comes up."

They smiled shyly at each other this time, but the silence returned. Jacob, who had lost all interest in the egg salad he was eating, tried desperately to focus his racing thoughts on something to say next.

When Rosalie smiled again, he actually felt the warmth hit him and he began to relax.

"And how do you like the story you're typing?" he asked.

Rosalie felt her throat tighten. She let out a little cough, then swallowed and forced herself to answer. She should say only positive things, she told herself. Being Rosalie, she just couldn't do it.

"I love your story; it's easy to read and flows very nicely, only…"she stopped there, realizing she had been about to say something unwise. She was grateful for this job, and although she had only been here a couple of days, she already loved working in this old house with this strange, but compelling man. She didn't want to jeopardize anything.

And indeed, she saw Jacob's posture stiffen just a bit.

Jacob had received a few bad reviews in his many years of writing, but he was not used to direct criticism. His agent said all literary critics were crooks and Jacob believed him. The author also had nothing to measure his accomplishments by, except for book sales, and based on those figures, he was a resounding success.

"Only what?" His voice was scruffy and low. He was staring down at his sandwich as if it had done the speaking.

Rosalie gulped slightly. "Only, nothing. I shouldn't have said anything, sir. It's not my place. You're a famous author, and I'm just your typist."

But her impulsive, honest self could not help adding softly, "I just meant your heroes are too perfect. They don't seem real sometimes. Roberto and Jacqueline are very similar to Davis and Geraldine in your last book."

Jacob looked up from his half-eaten sandwich to stare into her green eyes. He didn't seem angry, though, only curious and confused.

"As I explained when I hired you, I do not wish to be addressed formally. I'm Jacob, not 'sir.' Now, my heroes are alike?" he prompted.

"Yes. During this last week at home, I read several of your previous books to get a feel for what you do. You have a gift for putting words together; it's very easy to lose track of time when you're reading them, and your plots move along nicely. But the men all have rippling muscles and rough, egotistical attitudes, until they fall in love and change their wicked ways. They are always rich and live in mansions or on ranches they own."

Rosalie was losing herself now in the passion of her viewpoint.

"Meanwhile, the women are always kind, but afraid—afraid of the hero and usually afraid of something else, until they fall for that hero, the man who will protect them from whatever threatens them. Honestly, Jacob, I sort of feel I read the same book several times—the same two people always fall in love."

Jacob sat in silence, stroking his chin. His silence, however, alarmed Rosalie.

"I don't mean to find fault—you write so well; very nicely, in fact," she said in a rush of words. "And the settings and time frames are very different, of course. I really enjoyed reading them, Jacob."

Jacob pushed his plate away, having lost his appetite completely.

"My reading public certainly doesn't agree that the characters are not interesting," he said stiffly. When he looked at Rosalie, he saw alarm on her pretty face.

"Why don't you think my characters are real?" he prodded more gently.

Rosalie took a moment to think before choosing her words.

"Well… for example: with your heroines, you change the color of their eyes, hair, and their height. But they are always a size 4 with a petite build and 'round, firm breasts,' whatever that means. I always picture Barbie dolls—no faults, and kind of plastic." She reddened slightly.

But when she looked at Jacob, he appeared to be weighing her words. Emboldened by his concentration, she added, "Have you ever really seen such a woman?" She looked down at herself and added, "More of them look like me."

Jacob stood up from the table suddenly. "I think lunch is over."

Rosalie was sure that once again, she'd blown a job. "I'm sorry. I have trouble being too honest sometimes. I certainly didn't mean to offend you."

"Shocked me a little, yes. Offend me? I think not. I just want to mull over what you're saying. And maybe I'll go back and reread my books. In fact, why don't you take the afternoon off? I think I'd prefer to be alone today."

Rosalie shut her eyes and sighed. "And tomorrow?"

"I'll worry about tomorrow later, but yes, come in unless I call. I just need a few hours to think."

Jacob was at the dining room door.

Rosalie opened her eyes, gathered up her lunch remains, got up from the table, and peeked at the author's face as she passed him by, trying to assess how upset he was. She walked into the hallway, grabbed her sweater and issued a soft, "Call me if you change your mind. Otherwise, I'll be here bright and early tomorrow."

Jacob appeared not to be listening. He waved his hand in the general direction of the front door, and then turned to walk a few paces down the hallway. Just as suddenly, he turned back, his eyes quickly scanning her.

"And maybe you're right. My heroines should look more like you." He didn't wait for a response before turning and resuming his course.

Chapter 16

For the second time that day, Jacob pushed his plate forward on the dining room table. He'd never finished lunch, and now he had no appetite for the delicious dinner Mrs. Wells had prepared. Ever since Rosalie had left, he couldn't concentrate on anything except what she'd said.

He felt as if his foundation was crumbling. For most of his adult years, he had kept his life on an even keel; he was convinced he needed routine and control to counteract the lonely, violence-laden years when his father was the one in control. He found solace in writing beginning at an early age, and as an added benefit, his writing had been the one thing he'd done that had received approval from his father. Even at twenty, when Malcolm and Oswald had insisted that in order for his books to sell and become popular, Jacob had to include explicit sexual content, the author had developed a way to cope—he put his own fantasies down on paper. But were his stories just adult fairy tales with plastic characters? Bedtime stories for the lonely adults who couldn't face life as it really was?

"My God," he said aloud to his empty study, "why haven't I seen this before? I'm stuck writing to a formula—the same characters over and over."

He stood up and began pacing the room.

What should I do, though? Give up my writing? Go back to school at forty-five!

He was so intent on facing this new reality that he didn't hear the storm raging outside. The sun that had burned so brightly early in the day had been replaced by heavy clouds and downpour.

Jacob continued to pace, looking up only occasionally as lightning flashed. Somewhere in the distance, just as one of those flashes occurred, he heard a bell ringing. It didn't register with him for several minutes. The ringing finally broke through his reverie, however, and Jacob realized someone was at his front door.

A bedraggled Rosalie stood on the doorstep, thoroughly soaked. Her clothes stuck to her body like a second skin. She was so wet and cold that the nipples of her ample breasts were clearly evident through the gauze of the work dress she still wore.

"I am so sorry," Rosalie cried unaware of how she looked or how Jacob's body had reacted to her. She stood wrenching her hands, her mascara streaked and her hair wild.

"It was terribly wrong of me to criticize your books," Rosalie squeaked. "I'm just so stupid and impulsive sometimes. But I don't mean to upset or insult you with those words, and I do like this job. Your writing is truly beautiful, Jacob."

The author could see now that some of the moisture on her face was from tears that made her eyes glisten.

"Don't cry," Jacob said, completely at a loss of what to do. "There's no need to cry. Please just come in and get dry."

Jacob felt like he was in an unfamiliar world. What was this woman, who had left hours before, doing on his doorstep? He did not understand her at all; he didn't understand his own physical reactions to her, either. He itched to take her in his arms, stroke her hair and tell her she had been right… her words had hit home. But he had no right to touch her, and he had very little experience with lending comfort.

Instead, he said, "I don't know what you're apologizing for. There is nothing to forgive." He cupped one of her shoulders and gently pulled her inside.

"You told the truth as you see it. And I'm fine with that, truly."

He led her into the study where he'd lit a fire earlier, hoping the crackling inspiration would get his mind back on track to continue working on his book. Now, he led her to the fireplace and went into a nearby bathroom and grabbed an oversized towel. Once back in the study, he toweled off her hair, not really thinking about what he was doing, and then suddenly, he pulled away from the familiarity and wrapped the large towel around her shoulders instead. He pointed to a chair near the fire and said, "Sit."

Rosalie shook her head and whispered in a tiny voice, "I'm all wet. I'll get your chair wet."

"It doesn't matter. It will dry."

***

For the first time since she'd arrived on his doorstep, the dripping girl now looked into Jacob's eyes and felt a sudden jolt of realization. She saw a man grappling with deep emotions, and she thought she glimpsed fear. *Why is he afraid? I could understand anger, but fear?*

Jacob began to pace; Rosalie watched him. He walked back and forth in front of the fire, not seeming to see her or the room. He stopped several times and fiddled with the brass candlesticks that adorned the mantle. But he said nothing. He just resumed his pacing.

Rosalie had not yet sat in the chair, and she was beginning to feel the pregnant silence. She knew the man was saturated in his own thoughts and needed to let those thoughts escape. But she couldn't and probably shouldn't force him to talk.

"Have my comments about the book upset you?" she couldn't help asking.

Suddenly, he turned to her and stopped. He tilted his head as if listening and said simply, "No. I'm fine. Really. Please go home. The rain is letting up a little. I assure you, you've done nothing wrong, but I need to be alone right now. "

Rosalie couldn't believe he was telling her to leave. Again. Why did she keep making a fool of herself around this man? She turned so that he could not see the tears resume, threw back her shoulders and let the towel drop on the floor, and then headed for the door.

She was at the door, knob in hand, when she heard Jacob close behind her say, "I'm sorry." Rosalie stopped, but did not turn around.

"I just need some time to adjust and think," Jacob said softly. "Come back tomorrow morning and we'll have a long, productive day, I promise."

Rosalie turned back and finally realized she was not being fired. His chin was resting on his chest and he was scratching his neatly combed head.

His next words, however, surprised her.

"And if your schedule permits, perhaps we could go out to dinner and discuss a few things."

"Out to dinner?" she repeated, her voice shaky. Her question drew Jacob's attention back to her. His face came up; his deep blue eyes trapped her and held her completely.

"If your schedule permits," Jacob repeated, his voice gaining volume and certainty.

"That would be…lovely," Rosalie said as she finally escaped his gaze. She turned, opened the door, and left.

***

Once she was gone, Jacob returned to his study and sat in the chair Rosalie had never occupied. He steepled his fingers and rested his chin on the triangle of arm rests, arms, and hands.

Why had he asked his own secretary to dinner? He truly didn't know. He only knew that he wanted what was buried deep within him to be freed in some way that went beyond his usual twenty-seven chapters with at least three sex scenes and an apex of the action three quarters of the way through the book.

What was he going to do?

Chapter 17

During the work week, Rosalie usually buried her head under the covers when the alarm went off, hoping to stay as long as possible. This morning, however, her eyes popped open at the sound of the buzzer and she sprang from her bed.

She felt good, alive, and ready to face the day. It was such an unusual feeling so early in the morning; she was puzzled at its source.

I guess it's having a job I like, she thought as she stepped into the shower. With the water running full and hot, she began to sing, her voice soft and melodic.

"Oh, what a beautiful MORNing! Oh, what a bea-u-tiful dayyyy!" she sang, the silliness of the song making her laugh.

As she ran the pouf sponge down her body, it seemed to glide over her skin. The bodywash smelled delicious and flowery, the suds made her nose tickle. Today, the places where her flesh bulged simply didn't bother her.

What the heck is the matter with me? But as she stepped out of the shower, the realization hit her full force. It was the way Jacob had looked at her last night, after seeing her so bedraggled and wet. She had arrived furious at herself for what had come out of her mouth, but not so upset that she hadn't seen a tinge of lust and hunger in Jacob. The man had seen her clothes clinging to the curves that she hated so much, and he looked like he'd wanted to eat her alive. He hadn't said a word to indicate what he was thinking; she'd seen the desire in his eyes. And then, he'd asked her to dinner. Somehow, her big mouth, instead of getting her into trouble, had gotten through to him. He wanted her company past business hours, and at this point, she didn't even care if it was advice he wanted, or something more carnal. It was exciting to anticipate finding out.

Rosalie carefully chose what she would put on this morning. Something simple and colorful, she decided. No more all black or navy blue. She hooked a new bra she'd bought when she'd gotten the job over her generously apportioned breasts, noting that while the lingerie was neither fancy nor lacey, it felt good simply because it was fresh. She chose a pair of cotton panties that were the same off-white color as the bra. It wasn't that she felt her underclothes were important—she had no intention of having a sexual encounter with her new employer. But it was delicious to feel good on the inside, as well as on the outside.

Rosalie chose a flowing dress that would be both professional and appropriate for the evening's dinner. Over this, she buttoned the bottom few buttons of a tunic top covered with tiny yellow flowers and green leaves. She carefully applied a soft beige eye shadow, which matched her dress, and a thin line of eye pencil to outline her lashes, and then a little mascara to plump them up. She usually didn't bother with makeup unless it was a formal occasion. Today, it just felt right.

She peeked at herself in the dreaded full-length mirror and smiled.

"It doesn't matter how perfect you are, Rosalie," she shook her finger at the mirrored image. "It matters how you feel. He is going to take you out to dinner, and I'm pretty sure he's attracted to you."

She grabbed a light sweater, and left her room to face the world. She'd purposely set her alarm to get up before her mother because she didn't want a heavy breakfast and questions about her day. Just as she was about to open the front door, the phone rang and she grabbed for it, hoping she'd get it before her mother awoke.

***

Though Rosalie had enjoyed a blissful night of rest, Jacob had not been so lucky. He hadn't been able to sleep. He spent a few hours tossing and turning, his mind twisting and leaping from past to present. It seemed like his routine, his carefully laid out life, was somehow falling apart. The plots and characters of his novels were tired and stale. He took no solace in his statues, which were disappearing anyway. The hours of his day were interrupted by the daily presence of Rosalie. And while he had a successful writing career, he was no longer certain of why he'd become an author.

He'd finally gotten out of bed in the very early morning hours and tried to write. But the characters would not speak to him. With a few simple sentences, Rosalie had unnerved him. The hero of his book was too perfect with muscled arms and stoic bravery. His heroine was a china doll full of innocence, ready to break. *Of course she fell in love with the hero; she had no personality of her own!*

What do I know about how people really feel? Jacob kept asking himself. *I've lived in a box carefully built to protect me from the world and to keep me safe from disorder. I've crafted myself to be impenetrable. But why? Father is dead and Mother was practically dead when she was alive and breathing. I don't need protection from them anymore, and I never had their approval.*

Jacob had finally given up trying to write and fixed himself a whiskey and water—a rare action for a man who didn't even like the taste and hated the way alcohol caused people to lose control. He'd seen it too often in his own father. But Jacob drank the drink he prepared and even fixed a second one, which finally enabled him to relax.

A picture of Rosalie standing there before him, her wet clothes sticking to her body, popped into his head, and he felt his groin tighten. *What was wrong with him?* He'd certainly spent many hours writing about women's bodies and what they could do, but when he wasn't writing, he rarely thought about his heroines. Those women stayed safely on the pages of his novels. Somehow though, Rosalie felt very much alive and real and slightly dangerous. Just thinking about her sent a tremor down his spine.

Jacob had been a fool to ask her to dinner. The source of the impulse baffled the author. *What did he know about going to dinner with a woman?* He was forty-two and had probably been on ten official "dates" in the last two decades—awkward, formal affairs that ended with stiff goodbyes. He had no idea what to say to keep a woman entertained, and while several of the women had carried on lively conversations and then hinted of a liaison, he just hadn't been interested in keeping the evening going. He was not a stranger to sex—it could easily be purchased and completely discreet when you were rich. But dating? He'd sworn never to do it again.

This morning, with a slight headache and nothing decided he'd begun the process of soul searching and worrying all over again. By seven a.m., with Rosalie due to arrive in an hour, Jacob knew he was not ready to face her. When the clock finally reached seven-thirty, he dialed her number.

Chapter 18

The sun shining brightly through the old building's windows meant that Wretched would work tonight. It didn't really bother the boy; there hadn't been much to do this week—too much rain and he needed the two dollars Mr. Sir gave him every time a treasure was collected—Wretched had saved up almost enough to buy a pair of sneakers he'd picked out at the mall. Still, it was getting harder and harder to get through the space and the fear of not fitting kept the boy from eating. Wretched was used to hunger, just not to the extent this particular job required.

He reached into the cupboard and withdrew the bowl and cereal. He sighed. He was also tired of cereal. At least it was food he didn't have to beg for—he only needed to do what Mr. Sir demanded and Mr. Sir had promised there were only a few more times Wretched would have to get through that hole.

Maybe after this job is finally over, I'll take some of my money and buy bread and peanut butter, Wretched thought, as he filled his bowl. There was no powdered milk treat today and Wretched apologized to his kitten as he stroked the soft fur.

The boy sat down on his bed and slowly ate his breakfast, piece by crunchy piece. It didn't take long.

Wretched got up and rinsed out the bowl in the nearby bathroom. After returning everything to the cupboard, he straightened the covers on his bed.

He heard a noise outside his door and knew Mr. Sir had come to give him orders.

"Looks like a fine day," Mr. Sir announced, as he strode into the room. "It will be a good night to work and we haven't had one in awhile, so I want you to stick close today. No trips to the mall!" he said, rubbing his hands together. "I've got it all worked out so you can double up the amount of treasures we remove tonight."

"Oh, no," an alarmed Wretched exclaimed. "I can't get through that hole with two. I only had one last time and I dropped it, remember? The hole ain't big enough."

"I said I had it worked out, boy! And you don't have to remind me you dropped the statue," the man grumbled, drawing himself up and peering closely into Wretched's face. Wretched shrank away from the man's angry scowl.

Mr. Sir calmed down as he added, "I made a special holder so two of the treasures will be safe—it attaches to your feet. All you gotta do is slowly drag them out behind you. Once outside, you can get them out of the holder, put them in the safe pack and meet me at the usual place. Tomorrow, you can go to your damn mall or the park or wherever it is you go."

Wretched looked at the sock-like tool that Mr. Sir was showing him. It had two chambers and was made from thick material with a string on the end for attaching to his feet. The statues would be well padded and not touching each other.

It might work, the boy thought. "I'm frightened, Mr. Sir. I don't want to break the beautiful treasures."

"You better not even scrape them, boy!" Mr. Sir said loudly. "Or you know exactly what will happen."

Seeing the fear in the boy's eyes, the man changed his tone. He sat down on the bed and reached a hand out towards the boy, pulling the youngster forward by his arm until Wretched was at eye level.

"Wretched, this tool will work. I designed and tested it out myself," the man said in an even tone. "Just tie this to your feet at the door and drag the bundles gently behind you and nothing will go wrong. We're almost at the end of our work here and I'm upping your pay to six dollars tonight."

Wretched's fear dissipated. Six dollars was a fortune. Encouraged by the boy's excited eyes, Mr. Sir went on, "Try it now, boy. Tie them on and crawl across this room."

The man bent down and showed Wretched how to attach them securely to his feet. Then, with arms crossed, the man watched as the boy slowly wriggled to the other side of the room.

"Perfect," Mr. Sir exclaimed as he unwrapped the new tool from Wretched's feet. "That was just perfect, Boy. You'll be a rich man soon!"

Wretched tried to smile, but Mr. Sir wasn't looking. When the older man left the room, Wretched sat on his bed to think. Even though he was happy about the money, he was troubled. Too much could go wrong and he didn't really understand why he was taking someone else's treasures.

Two fat tears rolled down his face and the boy quickly wiped them away. He had promised himself, after the first time Mr. Sir had hit him, he'd never again allow the man to see him cry. He'd kept that promise to himself even this last time, when Mr. Sir had hit him particularly hard after he broke the treasure. Mr. Sir said he'd deserved it. Wretched was clumsy and stupid. He was little, and except for Mr. Sir, he had no one to look out for him.

Mr. Sir was not as bad as other people had been. Wretched was only six when Mr. Sir found the boy wandering the streets. The young boy already feared most grownups. He had run away from a group home because the head of the home had wanted him to do things—things that Wretched didn't understand; that didn't feel right. Mr. Sir yelled at Wretched a lot and occasionally hit him. But he didn't touch the boy in weird places. Now, Wretched was eight and considered himself a man. He knew he could not stay with Mr. Sir forever, but it was working for now.

Wretched stroked his kitten's fur as he thought back to the day Mr. Sir had found him. What a scared young kid he'd been. He'd gotten very lost in the city, terrified after some big boys chased him. Even after the boys were no longer in pursuit, Wretched had run and run. He had been so tired from running and so hungry from lack of food, that when he'd seen the man on the bench, deeply engrossed in a newspaper, with an unopened sack of fast food lying on the bench, the boy had grabbed the sack and tried to dash. Wretched still remembered how terrified he'd been when Mr. Sir had reached out and grabbed his wrist.

"What do you think you're doing?" Mr. Sir's voice boomed. He rose from the bench, the paper falling to the ground.

"I'm very hungry," the boy sobbed.

"Well, where are your folks, boy?"

"I ain't got none. Please don't hurt me," the boy cried and cowered.

Mr. Sir had relaxed his grip slightly, but held firm and peered closely into the boy's face.

"What's your name, boy?"

"I ain't got a name, Mister," the boy said, afraid that the man would haul him back to the group home.

"Then where's your home?"

"I ain't got a home, Sir."

Mr. Sir looked him over from head to toe, picked up his other arm, jiggled it, and then dropped it again.

"Pretty wretched being then, I'd say," said Mr. Sir, though the boy had no idea what a wretched was.

The man sat back down, dragging the child over to sit beside him and finally dropped the boy's arm. Wretched thought only, *This man isn't going to hit me.*

"Instead of trying to steal my food, Wretched One, how about if I have you work for me?"

"For money?" the boy whispered timidly.

"Yeah, kid. I can give you some money and more." The man then reached for the sack, opened it, took out a burger and handed it to the boy.

From that moment on, Mr. Sir had taken care of Wretched. He found him a place to sleep that was safe and usually warm, provided food that, until recently, wasn't limited by the job, and he even let the boy keep the stray cat that wandered into the building.

Most days, Mr. Sir was not angry and Wretched felt safe enough to stay. Although he'd have to stick close to his room today, he had his kitten, his two comic books and his locket to keep him company.

Wretched got up from the bed and found the crevice in the wall, reached inside and withdrew the locket. He knew it wasn't worth much money, but it was his own personal treasure. He used his dirty nail to open it. A woman Wretched did not know stared out at him. Once again, he smelled lilacs and felt the woman's arms around him. Wretched leaned back against his pillows and daydreamed about who she could be.

Chapter 19

"Is Rosalie McGovern there?" Jacob Hardy's voice came through the phone line as stiff and formal as the man often looked.

Rosalie had trouble matching that formal tone with the face she had been visualizing, which was Jacob with a smile. His call, however, made her frown. *Why is he calling this time?*

"This is she," Rosalie answered.

"Rosalie," Jacob said softly, a slight shakiness in his tone.

Oh boy, Rosalie thought. *What now?*

"Don't bother coming to work today."

Oh crap, oh crap, oh crap, Rosalie thought. The man had turned the tables yet again.

"I need the day to think. Just think."

Think about what, Rosalie wondered. *Whether or not to fire me? How to get out of dinner?* She looked down at her carefully selected flowery dress and sighed.

Jacob's voice had lost its shakiness when he continued, "I just need some quiet time today. I'm considering changing the direction of this book. I do still want to take you out tonight and maybe we can talk about it..." After a pause, he added, "That is, if you still want to go."

"Oh, yes." Rosalie hoped Jacob could not hear the excitement in her voice. "I'm looking forward to dinner."

"Then I'll pick you up at six-thirty. Is that all right?"

"Yes, Jacob. That's fine. I'll see you then."

She hung up the phone and sat down on the closest chair, her legs a bit unsteady. One phone call had crumpled the light feeling she'd had this morning. But she slowly let out the breath she'd been holding, while relief washed over her. The dinner was still on and what's more, she had the day off. She would take quiet time herself; finish the novel she'd begun reading before she started working, take a walk, and maybe soak in the tub. Then, when night approached, she would redo her makeup, do her nails, curl her hair, and put the flowered dress back on to have dinner with her new "friend."

***

Jacob placed the handset in its cradle and scratched his head. He really did not understand what he was doing. Only that he was acting bizarrely and that he felt a burden lifted. He was determined now to get some work done and he finally felt calm enough to attempt it. He walked into his study, eager to begin.

Six hours later, the fact he was going to dinner with a woman hit him in the face. "What a foolish waste of time!" the now-productive Jacob exclaimed. Why had he issued the invitation as a formal date? He went into his bedroom and opened up his closet. He needed to find something proper to wear. He stood staring at the closet's contents. A long line of gray and black expensive, well-cut suits he'd purchased from a merchant in Italy, which kept his measurements on hand, hung on one side of the closet.

"But they're all exactly the same," he cried out loud, throwing his hands up.

Jacob walked to the shelves and looked at his shirts—beige, white and a few blue, which he rarely wore. All were crisply pressed by the drycleaners and many were still in plastic, proving they had not been worn since coming back from the cleaners.

"A nice tie," Jacob said. But when he hit the mechanized tie rack that brought forth an array of two-hundred-dollar expensive silk creations, his shoulder sagged. They, too, were identical—black or navy, a few with stripes, most simply solid material. They were professional, but boring.

Jacob retreated from his closet, sat on his giant bed, and sighed heavily.

Even if he had something more appropriate or at least more casual to wear, where was he going to take her? He needed to make reservations, but the very few times he ate out were with his agent, a new publishing house, or the occasional editor or marketing person. Someone else usually made the reservations and most often they went to one of two private restaurants near where he lived, both obscenely costly. *Where did people go when they simply dined out?*

Jacob paced back and forth and then continued walking from room to room, hardly aware of what he was doing. He stopped in the great room in front of the giant picture window.

"This is ridiculous. Nothing is worth this grief," he said out loud.

When he looked outside the window, however, he saw Sam Osborne just getting out of his car and remembered the meeting he'd set up with the detective.

Geez, am I completely losing my memory, too? They had scheduled the mid-afternoon appointment to discuss the next steps in the investigation of the missing statues. Jacob, however, couldn't think about the blasted statues at the moment.

He threw open the front door and greeted the surprised detective with a handshake.

"I need help," Jacob said, drawing the detective inside by grabbing his arm.

Sam looked down at the arm and then back up at the man holding it.

"I don't have anything to wear," Jacob exclaimed, dropping his grip. "I don't know where to go to eat. I don't know what to talk about!"

Sam's forehead was wrinkled in confusion and Jacob realized how ridiculous he sounded. The author straightened his stance, stepped back and calmed himself.

"I'm sorry, Sam. I just need some advice. I am going to dinner tonight with my assistant Rosalie McGovern and I need a man's advice. I don't know what I should wear and I don't know where to take her. Too many of my suits are black or gray. I don't want to look like a funeral director."

Jacob sat down on an elaborate hallway bench. He ran both hands through his hair. The mussed hair fit well with the dark circles under the author's eyes.

"Black is a fashionable color, Jacob, and there is nothing wrong with gray, either," Sam said. "You just need something to liven them up. You could add some color by putting a bright-colored handkerchief in your pocket and matching that color with one of your ties. That would give your appearance a little spice."

"But I don't have any spice in my closet!" Jacob cried. He seemed to realize what he'd said and ran his hand through his hair again. Sam simply grinned and opened his cell phone.

"We'll order a tie, handkerchief and shirt from the Gentleman's Shoppe. I'm sure they will be more than happy to deliver this afternoon. What time is dinner?"

"I'm picking her up at six-thirty. I don't know what type of food Rosalie likes. Oh, God, I am such a mess. I can't believe I'm obsessing about a dinner. What's wrong with me?"

Jacob's tired, pleading eyes looked like they needed comfort more than advice, so Sam decided to be honest and supportive of this client he barely knew.

"It sounds to me like its more date than dinner. But Jacob, you're quite capable of pulling this off. You may keep to yourself because you like your privacy, but you do so by choice. I'm sure when you need to deal with the social aspects of being an author, you're fine."

Jacob looked over at Sam and thought both *he's right*, and, *who is this man? He's certainly not intimidated by wealth or fame.*

Out loud he said simply, "Okay."

Sam speed-dialed a number. "I don't date that often myself. When I do, I have a couple of favorite restaurants with good food, the right atmosphere, soft music and a fairly quiet place to talk. Let's make reservations at the LaSalle Café."

Sam spoke softly to whoever answered, and then pushed the end button and turned back to Jacob, "What color would you like from the Gentlemen's Shoppe?" he asked.

Jacob just looked dumbfounded, so Sam dialed a second number. "Is George working today? No, that's okay, I can talk to you. I need a tie, shirt and handkerchief that will dress up a black suit. Something not too outlandish, but that the ladies might like. Light green for the tie and handkerchief? Yeah, that would do. Use your judgment on the shirt color. Deliver it to four fifty-five Chester Lane, the Hardy residence, by no later than five. Jacob Hardy will pay you at the door."

Jacob sighed in relief. He was amazed at how easily Sam solved what just a minute ago had seemed a major problem. Sam's forthrightness gave the author the courage to ask for more advice. His eyes found Sam's.

"What will I talk about for several hours, Sam? I mean part of the reason I asked her to dinner was to discuss a new direction for my book. That probably won't take very long, though."

Sam laughed softly. "That one is easy, Jacob. And it doesn't matter whether it's a date or just dinner. Ask her about herself—her life at home, her friends, her hobbies. Don't be too nosey—you are her employer. But to get her talking, try thinking like you're interviewing one of your characters. You're interested in her for a reason. Find out what it is."

Jacob nodded his head up and down several times in approval of Sam's suggestions. *I can do this*, he thought. *Of course I can do this.* Jacob stood and shook off his nervousness.

"Thank you, Sam. I owe you a debt of gratitude. I need to make a quick call to my agent. But if you could find your way to the sitting room, I'll use my study, and then we can talk."

Chapter 20

Malcolm Sherburne's Santa Claus look was not enhanced by rage. Currently, his skin was a deep scarlet color that complimented the fire in his eyes.

Literary agents cannot afford to show their tempers in public—anger is not a profitable emotion. But he was alone in his big house now and he had just hung up the phone with his main breadwinner: Jacob Hardy.

"The nerve of that man!" Malcolm shouted. "After all the time I spent teaching him how to write to his audience, praising his every endeavor, and leading him down the path to riches… And now he says he is going to change what he writes! The stupid oaf knows nothing about what people will pay to read!"

Malcolm was wearing down a path in front of his desk, leaning slightly on his cane with every other step. Jacob had calmly explained in the call that he was going to take a break from the current book and maybe even change course with his writing altogether. Jacob wanted to explore the lives of what he called "real" people. The author would be missing his first writing deadline ever and that development did not fit into Malcolm's plans for his part of the income from that book.

"You son-of-a-bitch," Malcolm uttered. "What

the hell do you know of real people?_Your own father had to hire a damn prostitute just to teach you how to put sex in your novels! How dare you change our formula?"

Malcolm's pacing stopped, but only for a moment. Then the back and forth, back and forth resumed.

"You wouldn't know the slightest thing about making a buck if I hadn't held your damn hand every step of the way."

The agent looked up at the ceiling and shook his fist at the plaster.

"Oswald, you son-of-a-bitch. It was a helluva lot easier guiding your boy when you were around."

He shook his head and taking a deep breath, plopped into an armchair. He looked around at his home's rich furnishings and sighed deeply.

"What the hell am I going to do now," he whispered. "I don't make enough with my side job to keep this going."

***

Gregory Sterling was also pacing the floor of his study, deep in thought. But his face rarely turned red and his tall, gangling build and pinched face was more Lincoln than Santa Claus. He paused to rub his chin with one hand, his other arm held firmly behind his back. He walked to a bookshelf, picked up a picture and went to one of the chairs before the giant fireplace, sitting down with a sigh.

"How could you have turned out such an idiot for a son, Sis?" he asked the picture. "I thought he was just useless, but could he also be a thief?"

***

Catherine and Kevin Wells sat sipping afternoon cups of coffee. As was her custom, Catherine had delivered lunch to the author at exactly noon and then had come home to make a late lunch for Kevin. She'd spent the afternoon doing things around her own home, with Kevin getting underfoot most of the time.

"Why don't you ask Jacob if you can take on some of the yard duties," Catherine said in as casual a tone as she could muster. "After all, you're taking care of most of the flowering plants without Jacob even realizing it. Those flowers would have died this spring, if left up to Horace." She looked at him over the brim of her cup.

Kevin set his cup down a little too hard, spilling coffee onto the saucer. He glared at his wife, then picked up the paper and opened it without comment.

"I know Horace is doing the mowing, but he doesn't have your green thumb. And goodness knows, the place is big enough to have a lawn man, a garden man, and a car man," Catherine said softly.

Kevin flipped a page, his movements stiff.

"Kevin, darling. You've been home six months now. You know it's driving you crazy with only our small yard to work on! You pace the floor and the grounds at night, not able to sleep. You spend hours on our vegetable garden and you sneak over to pinch the buds and fertilize the plants whenever Horace isn't looking. I know it's not enough for you. Maybe Jacob can keep Horace for cutting grass and driving him around and let you help out with the bush and tree trimming, as well as the flowers."

Kevin sighed deeply and refolded the paper into quarters. He put it carefully down on the table beside his lunch plate and sighed again. He looked at the woman who had stood by him for so many years.

"I can't stand that no one will hire me, Catherine. And I've been proven innocent!"

"I don't care if you get paid, darling. We have survived just fine on my salary. But you need something bigger to focus on. You know how much Horace hates what he's doing in the yard. And I really believe Jacob always believed you were innocent! I don't think it would take that much to convince Jacob to split up the duties…"

Kevin stood abruptly, his fists balled in anger. Through clenched teeth, he muttered, "I don't need anyone's goddamn pity, Catherine. My name was cleared, but no one around here pays any attention to that fact. Who's going to give me back those three-and-a-half years, woman? Your saintly Jacob?"

He turned and walked out of the kitchen door.

His sharp retort appeared to have no effect on the stout woman, who rose and began clearing plates. She hummed softly as she worked, clearing the table and rinsing the few dishes. When they were in the dishwasher, she sat back down at the table and opened a well-worn recipe book.

"Maybe I'll try that Irish stew recipe that Jacob loves so much. Haven't done that one in a while…" She tilted her head and looked up from the book and towards the big house.

"Oh, wait, that's right. No supper tonight. The author has a dinner date with his secretary." Catherine chuckled softly, remembering how nervous Jacob had been at lunch when he'd told her he was going out.

"Maybe a night out will soften you up, buddy boy, and I can ask you about my Kevin," she said, closing the book.

Chapter 21

The minute Sam's assistant Casey heard the office door open, she called out to the detective, excitement evident in her voice. "Sam, I've run off those reports you wanted. I think you'll want to look them over, especially the one on Malcolm Sherburne." She was sitting behind a small oak desk clutching a half-inch sheaf of computer paper on top of a file folder. She put the papers in the file and then waved it in his direction, a smile on her face.

Sam walked to her desk for the file, went into his office and sat at one of two chairs in front of his desk to read. Casey wheeled her chair in after him, put the chair-lock on and picked up the cup of tea in the chair's holder. She sat sipping silently as Sam read the words. She hadn't offered Sam a cup of coffee because she knew his mind was already deeply embedded in the words before him.

Casey's report was based on information she had obtained with the help of Police Chief Robert McCoy, a personal friend of Sam's, as well as from a few calls between Casey and her police officer husband Danny. Sam had served with McCoy twenty years ago when the two were on the same Philadelphia police force. Chief McCoy had been appointed head of the Lancaster department at about the same time Casey's husband Danny had joined the force with the guidance and help from both men. Because of those two connections, Sam had quick access to public files and other information that would make most private investigators salivate. The Lancaster police force also trusted Sam, who never hesitated to help with local cases if assistance was needed.

Sam rubbed his chin as he read.

The jovial Mr. Sherburne had a record, although nothing very recent. He had spent a few years behind bars in the seventies for conning several elderly women. Malcolm had been in his late twenties then, and Sam picked up an old picture from the file. In those days, the man had been a handsome pixie—small with a wiry body, topped by a full head of rich brown hair. His long locks had the uncut look that hippies of that era wore and he sported a thick, long mustache.

Casey had combined the information from police reports, court case data, and news reports. They showed that Malcolm had hooked up with an older woman and lived with her for many months—first as a handyman, then as a lover. He ingratiated himself into her life slowly and eventually convinced her that he was her "soul mate." This lasted right up until the day the woman discovered her bank account was empty, her charge cards maxed out. She had testified against him in court, which resulted in his eventual conviction. He had made partial restitution and served eighteen months behind bars.

Even more puzzling to Sam was a recent incident. Malcolm had been arrested in connection with a questionable filmmaking operation, though the case had not resulted in a conviction for the agent. Malcolm had been present when police raided a "film studio." The raid came after several complaints were filed from property owners in an industrial park close to the run-down warehouse "studio." The legitimate business owners had tracked the comings and goings of the film crew and a hoard of "actors" and "actresses" who had created much noise, including a few screaming matches, outside the warehouse.

Police had enough evidence from the complaints to get a warrant to search the premises for possible violation of a business license. The raiding officers stumbled upon a pornographic film session. While Malcolm had been dragged in with the rest of the rowdy bunch to police headquarters for questioning, he'd received only a minor ticket for trespassing. The building's owners had no idea what was going on in the abandoned warehouse.

"Whoa," Sam said as he looked up at Casey. "It seems our Mr. Sherburne has a taste for the naughty." He sat scratching his head. Other than the racy content of some of Jacob's books, the detective couldn't see a connection, but the agent came across as sleazy and Sam was determined to look into him further.

Next up on Casey's report was Horace Montgomery, the groundskeeper at Jacob's estate. Horace had a few blemishes on his record, and they were mostly insignificant. He had been arrested once for drunk driving three years ago and had spent a night in jail for disorderly conduct last year. Even more interesting, though, was an arrest five years ago on a charge of fencing—selling televisions to a furniture store that later turned out to be a repository for stolen goods. The charges were dropped for lack of evidence.

"Fencing, huh," Sam looked up at Casey and grinned. "Well, that could be significant to the case."

Still, the charges had not stuck in court because the prosecutor could not prove the televisions were stolen, and Horace had served no time.

Kevin Wells, Catherine's husband, had not been so lucky. Kevin had been arrested for a robbery in a nearby neighborhood. He was convicted by a jury, mostly on circumstantial evidence and eyewitness accounts that placed him at the crime scene. Even though his wife and one neighbor had sworn he was at home, his resemblance to the real thief and some uncertain timing on the robbery was enough to get a conviction. It took almost three years and a new lawyer, who used DNA evidence, to clear Kevin's name.

Got to be some built up anger in that man, Sam thought.

The detective looked up at his assistant who blew on her nails and then rubbed them on her blouse, satisfied with what she'd been able to accomplish in a short amount of time.

"Okay, you get an A-plus for productivity. Anything else I should know?"

Casey's pretty green eyes sparkled. "Kevin Wells also was a school buddy of Oswald Hardy, Jacob's father," she said. "In fact, Wells, Malcolm Sherburne, and Oswald Hardy apparently hung around together in high school. Horace Montgomery also graduated from that class, though Aunt Matilda said she didn't remember seeing him with the Gang of Three, as the other three boys were nicknamed. I guess the guys were real mischief-makers, though they never got into trouble with the law. Oh, and Kevin served as the Hardy gardener until he was convicted—then Horace Montgomery took over. How's that for yet another twist?"

"Wow," Sam exclaimed, "You've been a busy girl today, Casey. How the heck did all that come out from the police reports?"

"It didn't, Sam. A quick look into the high school yearbook showed the three of them together in several pictures. They were all on the football team, and Oswald was the star. Anyway, I recognized one of their classmates, my 'Aunt' Matilda. She's not really my aunt by blood, but she's Sarah's sister."

The Sarah that Casey was referring to had raised Casey after her parents had died in a tragic car accident. She and her husband, Joseph, still lived with Casey and Danny and took care of their baby, Gus.

"I called Matilda and had a lengthy chat with her about her school days. Oswald was quite the ladies' man, but never kept a girlfriend for very long. He apparently had a reputation for meanness. Malcolm used to hang on his every word, though—kind of his own personal fan."

"And Kevin Wells?"

"She remembers seeing the three of them

together, but doesn't really remember much about Kevin other than he was the quiet one and that he was nicer than the other two."

"Sometimes it's the quiet ones that end up being dangerous," Sam said. "And did you check around about Gregory Sterling, the art dealer?"

"I made a few calls. He apparently has a reputation as a shrewd businessman. He's not well liked at all—not here and not in his own town. However, I found no reports or rumors of criminal activity. Sterling and Company seems to have an impeccable reputation."

"I'm certainly not surprised no one likes the man," Sam grumbled, remembering the unpleasant interview. He looked up from the file Casey had given him, smiling broadly.

"Well done, Casey. I'll turn you into a detective yet," Sam said.

Casey smiled in return and Sam felt again the warmth this young woman brought to his life every day. She wheeled back to her desk and Sam bowed his head to study the reports in more detail. After a half hour, his head popped back up and his thoughts returned to Jacob Hardy. He hoped the dinner was going well. Sam shook his head as he remembered how nervous Jacob had been. *He really must have lived like a hermit these past few decades*, Sam thought. *The man was in his forties, but had acted like a nervous teenager this afternoon.*

Sam chuckled softly. Although Jacob had said it was just a dinner, Sam suspected it was more than that for the author. The detective hoped it worked out between the author and his assistant. The man certainly needs something in his life besides little statues that keep disappearing.

Chapter 22

As soon as she heard a car in the driveway, Elizabeth McGovern ran to the living room window to peek out. She parted the curtain slightly to get a better look. "Oh my," Rosalie's mother gasped. "He's driving a very shiny black Lincoln!"

"Come away from the window, Mother," Rosalie said with more force than she normally used with her mom. "He'll see you staring out at him."

After getting a quick glimpse at Jacob, Elizabeth reluctantly let the curtain fall back into place. "He's very good looking," she said, a note of surprised pleasure evident in her tone.

The mother had her hand on the doorknob before the doorbell sounded. She threw open the front door and gave an enthusiastic, "Come in, Mr. Hardy, come in!"

When Jacob paused on the doorstep, looking confused, Elizabeth grabbed him by the arm and pulled him inside.

"I'm Elizabeth McGovern, Rosalie's mother. So glad to meet the famous writer!" she said. Once he was inside, Elizabeth let go of Jacob's arm and grasped his hand for a vigorous pump.

Jacob swallowed, uneasy with the familiarity and uncertain how to react. Although he'd suffered through book signings, his picture wasn't even on the book flap, and he did not conduct the interviews that so many other writers use to sell their books. He knew his name was famous, but he had no desire to be recognized in public.

"I'm Jacob Hardy," he said. Realizing she'd already said his name, he cleared his throat and added, "Pleased to meet you, Mrs. McGovern."

Elizabeth turned a pretty pink, her eyes lighting up as the "famous" Mr. Hardy said her name.

Rosalie knew it was time to take charge of the situation before her mother further embarrassed her boss.

"I'm ready to go, Jacob," she said calmly as she grabbed a lightweight coat from the sofa. Jacob took the coat from her, shook it out slightly, and then held it open for Rosalie to slip into.

"Oh my," gasped Elizabeth. "Such a gentleman."

As Jacob and Rosalie moved towards the door, Mrs. McGovern followed closely behind. "You'll call, dear, if you're out past midnight? You know I worry about you."

Rosalie rolled her eyes behind her mother's back. She glanced sideways at her dinner companion and saw a slight smile on his face. Rosalie stopped long enough to turn around and say, "Have a good evening, Mother. I'll call if I'm going to be very late."

Jacob and Rosalie could feel Elizabeth's eyes on

them as they walked to the car. The mother watched until both were behind seat belts. When she closed the front door, Rosalie and Jacob sighed in unison.

Jacob started the big car and drove for one block. He then pulled up to the nearest curb and stopped.

Rosalie's head snapped around to stare wide-eyed at him. "Don't tell me you've changed your mind and are taking me home already!"

Jacob chuckled softly. "I guess I deserve that remark. But no, I'm not cancelling dinner. I just wanted to ask you if you'd mind driving this behemoth. I managed to get to your house with only a few near misses, but I honestly haven't driven a car much in twenty years. I don't really have a need. I don't travel much and I usually hire a car or have Horace, my yard man, drive me."

Rosalie smiled, sat back, and ran her hand along the rich leather interior.

"I'd love to drive this beautiful vehicle, Jacob."

"If you don't mind then, I think we'd be safer with you behind the wheel."

Rosalie laughed out loud, the features of her face relaxing completely. "Of course, Just Jacob," she teased and opened her door. They got out and exchanged places. When they were settled in their new seats, she asked, "Where to?"

"The LaSalle Café on 24th and Maple. I have directions here if you don't know the place." Jacob reached into his pocket and withdrew a small piece of paper. "Sam wrote them down for us."

"Sam?"

"Sam Osborne—the detective who's looking into the thefts. He happened to stop by the house… and I… well, I asked him a lot of questions."

"Isn't he usually the one asking questions?" Rosalie asked. "What did you need to know?" She reached across the small space between them and took the paper to study its contents.

Jacob's handsome features were momentarily spoiled by discomfort.

"You'll laugh if I tell you."

Rosalie's intense gaze left him no choice but to continue.

"I'm afraid it had to do with something to wear and where to go. I've been lacking lately in social engagements."

Rosalie's expression remained serious. "Maybe I'll laugh, Jacob. But I hope to laugh with you. I would never laugh at you. I'm just curious what you needed to know."

She put the paper with the address on the console where she could easily reach it and started the car.

"How about we get to the restaurant and I'll fill you in," Jacob said.

They drove the next ten minutes in silence, but it was a relaxed lull. Rosalie loved the feel of the big automobile and savored the way it handled. She kept her eyes on the road, glancing at nearby buildings so she didn't miss their destination. Jacob just stared at the buildings they passed, lost in thought.

"Darn," Rosalie said after another few minutes. "I may have already gone by it. I'll circle this block, but can you look for 502 Maple for me?"

Jacob snapped back into reality and glanced over at Rosalie, then gazed out the window, studying the buildings and calling out the occasional number.

Rosalie drove around the block and when they were back on the main road, slowed and finally drove up to a front entrance.

"502 Maple. You found the place!" Jacob said, as if Rosalie had accomplished a great feat.

A valet came out, opened the driver's door and took the keys from Rosalie as she and Jacob got out of the car.

They walked under a long awning and past the doorman holding the door, who gave a slight bow as they entered. Once inside, Jacob gave the host his name and the couple was ushered to a table in an alcove facing out to the rest of the tables. It was a perfect spot to observe others, but still have some privacy.

A waiter approached almost immediately, a long, narrow leather menu in his hand.

“Wine, monsieur?” the sommelier asked.

“No,” Jacob said without thinking. Then he remembered his manners and turned to Rosalie. “I’m sorry. I don’t drink much, but perhaps you would like something?”

“Thank you, Jacob. Sometimes I like a glass of wine, but tonight I feel like iced tea.”

By this time, the sommelier had been replaced by a smiling waiter. He introduced himself as “Louis” and turned to Rosalie. “Would you like lemon with your iced tea, madam? And Sir, would you care for a beverage?”

“Iced tea for both of us,” Jacob said.

The waiter left to fetch their drinks, and the author and his companion looked down at the menus Louis had left behind. They were written in French and neither Jacob nor Rosalie admitted it right away, but they had no idea what was available to order. Louis came running back to the table almost immediately and handed them two stiff pieces of paper. “My apologies, Mr. Hardy, Ms. McGovern,” he said. “Mr. Osborne asked me to give you these. I’m afraid I almost forgot.” Jacob and Rosalie looked down at the papers and were relieved to see English staring back up at them. The list had certain entrées highlighted and Jacob realized Sam must have given the staff his recommendations.

“Wow. That Sam thinks of everything!” Jacob said with a laugh.

“I guess you have a new friend, or at least a

new older brother," Rosalie said.

Jacob looked surprised at her words. He sat back in his seat and said nothing. Instead he picked up the English menu and the two began discussing possibilities.

After they'd made their selections and told the enthusiastic Louis what they wanted—Cornish game hens stuffed with cranberry rice for Rosalie, filet mignon with baby potatoes for Jacob—Rosalie smiled and asked, "What else did Sam think of, then?" She was staring at her own folded hands on the table, but from the corner of her eye she could see Jacob's sheepish expression.

"Just about everything. I'm sorry, Rosalie, I'm afraid I don't have much experience planning a dinner out. Sam picked out this restaurant, made the reservations, helped me choose what to wear, and even ordered this tie and handkerchief." Rosalie looked at his face and could see that he was uncomfortable.

"I'm afraid I'm used to having others plan the details," Jacob said.

He ran his hand over his face, as if to clear away the unpleasantness of embarrassment. He chuckled softly and withdrew another slip of paper from his breast pocket. "Sam even gave me a list of things to talk about. Do you want to see it?"

"Oh, no," Rosalie said, her eyes twinkling. She looked very much like she was trying to hold back a laugh. "I think we're doing just fine on our own. Besides, a little silence is sometimes nice."

And silence was what came next. But again, the lull was comfortable as the two sat sipping their teas and watching the other people in the restaurant.

"She is *not* in love with her dinner companion…"

"Pardon me?" Jacob said, his eyes widening as he turned to stare at Rosalie. But his eyes followed hers to the table that had caught her attention. A woman sat in stony silence, staring down at her food as her dinner companion rattled on and on.

Jacob turned his head in another direction and discreetly pointed to a table where a very fat elderly man was talking and eating at the same time. His equally grey-haired companion, unlike the woman at the first table, was listening in rapt attention.

"He is a widower with fifteen grandkids, and she always wanted children. This is their first date."

Rosalie then nodded her head towards a table caddy-corner from theirs. "She is a hard-nosed executive, celebrating a new contract with an underling. She's drunk, but it has nothing to do with the martini and everything to do with a sense of power."

Jacob nodded in the same direction and Rosalie saw a man at a table just behind the executive. He was eating alone, slowly savoring whatever was in his mouth. "His wife thinks he's working late. But he's having an affair—with the food. He'll go to the gym next and work off those extra calories…"

And so on it went, until the waiter delivered two steaming, artistically adorned plates of food. The two ate quietly, savoring their delightful choices and enjoying the taste of foreign food on their tongues. The few words they exchanged centered on what they were enjoying and neither looked uncomfortable. After ordering coffee, however, Jacob turned to Rosalie, a look of determination on his face.

"I'd like to know more about how to make my characters real. I know I've lived too long in my little cocoon, wrapped in my wealth, confident in my writing. But I took to heart your comments and would like you to elaborate. Do you have any ideas on how I could do that?"

Rosalie's brow wrinkled slightly. What could she tell this man, who had lived so long as a recluse? Putting her cup down gently on the saucer, she took a few moments to collect her thoughts.

"I think what you need is inside of you, Jacob. You just showed me with the little game we played. You just need to bring it out more in your writing."

Jacob only looked confused.

Rosalie looked around the room. "You brought these characters to life, Jacob, adding a dimension to them by giving them a story. You don't really know that couple or that woman. Your mind made up who they were. You can do the same with your characters. Instead of being focused on fitting them into your planned plot, let them be human and make their own mistakes."

"You mean play our little people game with my own characters?" Jacob asked.

"Yes," Rosalie said her tone now excited. "That's just what you need. Let's try it. Look around, expand on your quick analysis and make up what happens to them based on who you made them out to be."

Jacob tilted his head to let the idea sink in.

"How about..." Rosalie nodded her head towards a table to their right, a little less in their line of vision. "Turn to your right—as if you were looking for the waiter—and look at that table beside us."

He did as directed and then turned back to her. "An elderly man and a very young girl. I suppose he could be her sugar daddy, though she looks a little bored," Jacob said.

"The man is indeed wealthy. But he's in the midst of a nasty divorce," Rosalie began. "Part of the agreement is that he must take his daughter for one weekend a month. This is the first weekend, and within the course of the first few hours, he's realized he doesn't know his own flesh and blood. He never paid her much attention—he was too busy earning money."

Rosalie's eyes narrowed just a bit. "The daughter doesn't want to be here at all. In fact, she had to turn down a date with a boy she's been trying to get to ask her out. To her, dining in a foreign restaurant with someone that has nothing in common with her, is a disgusting turn of events. What she doesn't know is that if she'd gone out with that boy, she'd be in danger. The young man is plotting to kidnap her and has been posing as a new transfer student waiting for his opportunity to connect with the girl."

Jacob's jaw dropped. "Hey, maybe you need to be the writer here! How on earth did you come up with all that?"

Rosalie laughed. "I don't write well, Jacob. But I have an active imagination all the same, as do you. I've seen it in your writing. You came up with all those plots and descriptions that keep so many people reading your books. I just think you need to stretch that imagination to write something a little more challenging with characters that are more complicated. Your creativity needs some exercise."

She looked around the room.

"Okay, your turn. Take the couple that just sat down directly across from us."

"Oh, I can't presume to know what they do," Jacob protested.

"Of course you can presume. You did that earlier with the other people. You don't have to know for certain who they really are. You have to create their stories based on the characteristics you've given them. Pretend these two are your characters and make up a story."

Jacob took a closer look at the couple. He glanced at Rosalie and then back to the couple.

"Well," he began, "Gaston and his date Lucille are celebrating the night they met, which was six months ago. Lucille insisted they celebrate in this restaurant, where they first fell in love. Gaston, however, is very uneasy. He's a married man, and Lucille is not his wife. In fact, Lucille believes Gaston is splitting up with his wife. Gaston, however, knows differently. At the moment, he is desperately afraid that someone he knows will see them together, and he's already thinking about a back-up story in case their rendezvous gets back to his wife—something about running into an old girlfriend. Gaston knows he's taking a chance, but he's agreed to come here because Lucille has threatened to break up with him and he's not ready to do that. He really wants to keep her in his life, but he can't afford to divorce his wife—unless, of course, he can find a way to make her end up dead."

"Oh, that's wonderful!" exclaimed Rosalie. "Let's try another."

The two of them proceeded to fine-tune the game they had created. They sat drinking coffee and story making for more than an hour; the time broken up only by the delivery of a dessert they decided to split after the fifth time Louis asked politely if there would be anything else.

Finally, Louis announced that it was eleven p.m. and the restaurant was closing. Sometime during the last twenty minutes, the conversation had edged away from the make-believe and into the tentative first getting-to-know-yous. Jacob shared with Rosalie how he'd become an author—he'd been writing since he was a young boy, lost in a world of putting words together to create an image. But becoming published had happened gradually, pushed along by his father and Malcolm Sherburne. Rosalie shared the frustrations she'd had at trying to find a job that both kept her interest and let her exercise her brain. She shared her love of literature, and her regret at not being able to find a way to use it to support herself.

Outside, the air had taken on a pleasant coolness. Rosalie drove towards her home, parking a block away so her mom couldn't see the car. The author and his assistant had agreed a short walk on this lovely evening was a must.

At Rosalie's door, the first feeling of awkwardness took over. Jacob took her hand for just a second and then dropped it as if it were hot. They both said a stiff good night; Jacob turned and walked away. He had gone only a few paces when he turned and looked back.

Rosalie stood as tall and smooth as one of his statues. A streetlight illuminated her shapely figure and the dark of her hair seemed to absorb some of the light; the reflection off the door behind her glowed like a halo around her head. He couldn't see her eyes, but he felt her calmness and contentment.

He walked back to her without thinking and bent to plant a kiss on her cheek. Her palm flew to the spot he'd kissed, but she didn't seem upset with him.

"I'll see you tomorrow at work," he said.

She smiled then and Jacob's heart lurched.

"I'll be there every morning that you don't tell me to stay home."

Jacob only chuckled and left.

As he got into his car, he said to himself, "Never again will I tell you to stay away."

Chapter 23

Sam's knock on Jacob's door the next morning summoned a smiling Catherine, who led the detective towards a breakfast nook near the massive kitchen, explaining as she went that Jacob had invited her into the house to set up breakfast—had even invited her to dine with him. Her voice was laced with awe, as if the author's request was out of character.

Jacob was dabbing his mouth with a linen napkin. "Thank you, Catherine. That was a particularly delicious quiche. Sam, I'm sure Catherine wouldn't mind heating some up. Would you like to try her excellent cooking?"

Sam noted the broad grin on the author's face. *The evening must have gone well*, he thought.

"I ate already, Jacob, but thank you. Perhaps I'll get a sample some other time. I was wondering if you'd mind if I take a closer look around the property. I keep returning to the fact that there has to be some way the burglar can get in," Sam said.

"Indeed, have a look around," Jacob said. But his light, easy tone was followed by a scowl.

"We had another robbery last night," Jacob said. "This time, the thief took two of my statues."

Sam's eyes widened, surprised that the news about the statues had not been the first words out of the author's mouth. "Wow, Jacob. And you didn't hear anything at all?" He sat down caddy-corner from Jacob.

Jacob shook his head. He'd already lost the scowl. Instead, his brow was wrinkled in puzzlement.

"It's very odd, really. I would assume the thief came after I went to sleep like the other times, though I didn't check the statue room until this morning. I was up pretty late, so wound up from my dinner that I couldn't go to sleep."

"Anyway, I went into the study and wrote until almost three a.m. I don't think I heard anything, but by then I was pretty tired and not thinking about the statues. Like I said, I never checked on them. I just went into my bedroom and zonked out."

Sam didn't look up from his notebook as he asked, "I guess the dinner went well, then?"

Jacob sighed loudly, drawing the detective's curious eyes up from his notebook. The author appeared to have completely forgotten the thefts and was staring off into space.

"It couldn't have been better."

He brought his attention back to the detective.

"My thanks to you for helping out, Sam. You certainly went above and beyond the call of duty. Rosalie and I were astonished that you thought of the menus in English. And we both went with your recommendations. It was an excellent and productive evening. I owe you a debt of gratitude. "

Sam smiled warmly. "We all need help once in a while, Jacob. Whether it's advice on what to wear, or help with a case."

The detective tilted his head. "In fact, I know you're busy with your work this morning. Since Mrs. Wells is here, do you think I could get some help with this house search?"

Sam turned to the housekeeper/cook when he mentioned her name and noticed that her expression was almost as relaxed and content as Jacob's.

"You know the house as well as anyone, besides Jacob," Sam said to her. "I could use a tour guide this morning."

"Why, Mr. Osborne, I'd be delighted. I could let you in on the history of the place as we go. Jacob?"

"Of course, my dear. Of course," Jacob said heartily. He rose and put his napkin on the plate and then retired to his study, a look of determination replacing the dreaminess.

***

Catherine's light mood continued as she led Sam through the house, chattering the whole way. Although Sam suspected the housekeeper knew about the dinner, she respected her employer's privacy enough not to gossip about the author's apparent happiness. Instead, her natural inclination to jabber took the form of the weather, the house's many fine attributes, and its former occupants.

They started upstairs, and Sam checked every window and peeked into and behind closets, looking for clues. He knocked on walls seeking a secret passageway, but Sam didn't really expect to find anything on the second level as the thefts were occurring on the first floor. Jacob's bedroom was on that floor and all the windows were locked up tightly.

In one of the bedrooms, Catherine paused and her light mood darkened with an expression Sam interpreted as sorrowful. He glanced around the room, seeing a very feminine setting with an eyelet comforter on the four-poster bed and two matching grand antique dressers along one wall. The room was furnished in pastel pinks with splashes of forest green.

"This was Millie's room," Catherine explained. "I spent a lot of time in this room for the decade and a half after she married Oswald and before she died. I'm afraid the poor woman didn't have much of a life. She was much more of a recluse than Jacob. Millie was only happy in this room, reading a book, playing with her little dog, or watching soaps. Jacob would visit, but only occasionally, and she usually didn't have much to say to the boy, though I know she loved him dearly."

Sam was about to push for more information, but Catherine shook her head slowly, then left abruptly. Sam took a final look around the room, amazed at how beautiful it was and how useless the beauty, sitting in silence, had become.

Downstairs, Sam repeated his thorough search. He checked all the windows for signs of entry, crawled into cupboards and knocked on the back panels, and then knocked along the walls to listen for echoes. He also went into the basement with a flashlight that Catherine provided. He was covered in dust when he finally emerged from that search and after a quick wash-up, Catherine invited Sam into the kitchen for coffee. Jacob remained in his study, the door closed.

Catherine's endless chatter had continued as she walked through the house with Sam; most of it had to do with the house. Now, sipping coffee, Sam tried to bring the conversation around to a topic that might help with his investigation.

"How's your husband Kevin doing reentering the world outside prison?" Sam asked Catherine.

The housekeeper's face looked momentarily sad again, but she sighed and seemed to draw herself up as she replied, "He's trying very hard to adjust, but it's difficult when you have no job and few friends. The people he knew well before he went into jail are no longer friends. Too many gave up on him. I think most of the people in this community, and in our own neighborhood, considered him guilty. I was his only visitor while he was in that place—even his so-called buddy, Horace, never bothered to visit. I think my Kevin was deeply wounded by how people treated him and I'm sure it will take some time to start healing."

"I didn't realize Kevin and Horace were such good friends," Sam said.

"Well, they hung around together, that's all. They played poker once in awhile. Went to the track. You know—guy stuff.

"When they were all in school, Oswald was also a friend of his. He distanced himself as he got richer and richer. By the time he hired my Kevin for the groundskeeper job and Horace for the occasional odd job, the men had become simply employer and employees," Catherine added.

"But the three were close in high school?" Sam prodded.

"Not Horace, no. But Oswald, Kevin and Malcolm Sherburne were jocks together and socialized for a while after high school. Oswald inherited some money at a young age when his own dad died and he was well-off even in high school. Back in those days, and even after he married Millie, he was pretty generous when it came to the boys he hung out with. Can't say the same when it came to his own wife." She shook her head. "Even though by then, a lot of his wealth was coming from Millie's inheritance. This house is actually the one she grew up in."

"Oswald was not generous with his own wife?" Sam prompted.

Catherine got up to pour more coffee into her cup, even though it was at least half full. When she came back to the table, she offered Sam a warm-up and then sat down again, placing the pot in front of them.

"Oswald changed a lot after he married Millie," Catherine said, lost in the past. Sam's attention was drawn to her face. "How did Oswald change?"

"Well, he'd never been what you'd call nice. Had a bit of a mean streak, even back in high school. After he pursued and won the hand of one of the richest bachelorettes in Lancaster and moved into her house, he became downright cruel. I don't mean physically abusive, though I suspect he may have hit the boy in the early years. But he did other things to Millie that were just plain vicious."

"Oh?" Sam prodded.

"He found every occasion in the world to deride her. I think she retreated to her room so she wouldn't have to face his insults and screaming. Poor Millie. She just hadn't been raised in a house of screaming, and her bedroom became a safe zone. At least after what happened to Buttons."

"Buttons was Millie's dog?" Sam deduced.

Catherine wrapped her hands around the bottom of her coffee cup as if she were seeking the warmth of the coffee inside.

"Buttons was a lovely miniature white poodle and Millie adored her. The dog had been a gift from her father, who passed away just before Millie and Oswald married. Millie doted on that dog—even more so than her own child, who was born just a year after the wedding."

Her eyebrows wrinkled in a scowl. "Oswald couldn't stand Buttons' yapping. The dog was not allowed on the second level of the house, until Millie put her foot down and demanded a room of her own. She had a doggie door installed off the kitchen, so Buttons didn't even have to bark when she wanted to be let out or in."

Catherine's cheeks heightened in color, reflecting her anger.

"Even that wasn't good enough for Oswald. One day, the dog just disappeared. Millie was heartbroken and wouldn't come out of her room for several days. Oswald blamed it on the doggie door, but we all knew he simply got rid of the dog."

Sam wasn't focused on how cruel Oswald was, however.

"A doggie door?" he said aloud. "There was a doggie door?"

***

"I can't believe I didn't see this," Sam told Catherine as he bent down to inspect the doggie door, which was built off of a large mud room/laundry room attached to the kitchen.

"It was made to look this way, Sam—invisible to the naked eye. When Millie demanded the door, Oswald paid a specialist to build it like this."

"Funny, Jacob didn't mention it on that initial grounds inspection." Sam bent down to run his fingers around the area where Catherine had indicated. He could feel the indentation where wall became door, but it was invisible to anyone standing up. The door did not budge when Sam pushed against it.

"I doubt Jacob thought of it. He may not even know about it. The thing hasn't worked in years," Catherine said. "I assumed Oswald had nailed it shut or spackled it; somehow sealing it from the outside."

Sam didn't think so. The door wouldn't move, but his sensitive fingertips could feel just a slight chill around where the indentation was.

"I'm going to look at it from the outside," Sam said.

He went back into the kitchen, out the door and around to the side of the house. He had to work his way through very thick bushes to reach the door. He crouched down and saw that the bushes were less dense at the ground level. Sam sat down on the ground and ran his hand along a piece of plywood. He could just get his fingers under the side of the wood, which he discovered was loose in its place. The board of plywood was resting against the house and held there by several rusty, bent nails at the bottom and one at the top.

Thinking about fingerprints, Sam got out his handkerchief and wiggled one of the bent nails at the bottom until it came free. Now, he could see how the plywood could easily be removed.

Sam worked his way back out of the thick bushes. He stood, stretched, and then took his handkerchief out of his pocket, looking down at his find. He saw what looked like blood on the nail. Back in the kitchen, he got a plastic bag from Catherine for the bloody nail and handkerchief.

"This definitely looks like it could be our point of entry," Sam said to Catherine. "But I don't see how a person could get through that hole. It was built for a small dog."

"My goodness," Catherine said, her eyes wide, her voice excited. "Do you suppose someone has trained a dog or maybe a monkey to steal Jacob's statues?"

Sam chuckled. "That would be one very smart animal. No, it's pretty surprising how someone trained to get through small places can maneuver their bodies to fit."

He looked down at the blood on the nail.

"I'm afraid this person had some difficulty getting through recently."

Chapter 24

When Rosalie appeared at work later that morning, her boss was at the door to greet her. He had told her to sleep late. Now, he handed her a tape to transcribe.

"I couldn't sleep last night, so I got up and dictated for several hours and finished this morning. Tell me what you think as soon as you get it typed up," Jacob told Rosalie, then turned abruptly and left the hall.

Rosalie took no offense; she was beginning to know the author and his quirky ways. She knew that his nervousness meant that what he'd dictated was important to him. She looked down at the tape, realizing he'd put in some serious time last night and this morning. The recording was near the end of side B, which meant he'd put in ninety minutes of talking that would have, in reality, taken several hours to perfect. The author's assistant hurried upstairs to find out what the writer had created.

As she typed, her excitement increased. The story was much different than the one she'd been working on and two hours flew by as she became engrossed in the tale of the disfigured man who lived in a castle, shut away from the world. This story had a heroine like in his other books, but so far, she had been a source of strength for the hero, which was very unlike the porcelain-veneered women in Jacob's usual romances.

As soon as she came down to eat lunch, Jacob peppered her with questions. "Well, what do you think? Is my story more interesting?"

"Oh, definitely," she replied as she sat down close to him at the table, this time without an invitation. "It's much better, Jacob." She gave him a warm smile.

"But something is not quite right," he said anxiously, studying her face. "I can tell by your voice."

Although she didn't want to upset her employer, Rosalie knew she should be honest with her new friend. He genuinely seemed to value her opinion.

"The tale is truly engrossing; a man shut away in a castle, a heroine who stands up to people who call him a monster. It's a good story, Jacob," she said softly. "But don't be afraid to bring out the feelings of your characters—even if the man is bitter and the woman insecure. The events that have occurred so far in the tale are engrossing and intriguing, but the interaction between your characters reads stiffly because we don't understand why they are doing what they do. We need to get inside their heads."

Jacob was nodding, his food untouched.

"That having been said, getting into their heads can be the fun part, Jacob. These characters are much more real than those in your old books, and I like their flaws. The heroine is a bit of a flake, isn't she? But she's funny. And the hero is still a he-man in many ways, but he's been badly hurt in his life. As a reader, I want a glimpse of how he thinks."

"Then what do I need to do, Rosalie?" Jacob asked anxiously. He didn't seem upset, just curious. He finally picked up his fork.

"You need to show why they are doing what they do. It doesn't need to come out all at once—maybe just bit by bit. Insert what you would feel if you were them and it was all happening to you."

"You mean work on bringing out their motives, like we did with the characters we made up in the restaurant?" Jacob said, rubbing his chin with his free hand. The fork in the other hand had still not made it to the plate of lasagna before him.

"Yes, Jacob." Rosalie opened her sack to take out the sandwich she'd packed.

"Say, I've got an idea," she said, before taking the first bite. "Why don't we go over to the mall this afternoon and just sit there and observe people, like we did during our meal. We'll add something to our game—what they might be thinking!"

Jacob raised his eyebrows in surprise. "The mall, huh? I don't believe I've been to the mall except for once at the big book store where I did a signing ten years ago." He began to pick at his meal with the fork as he thought. Suddenly, he looked up at Rosalie and grinned. "But if you say it's time for a field trip, I say, let's go for it!"

Jacob got up and went to the sideboard for another plate. He dished out more steaming pasta and returned to the table to offer it to Rosalie, along with a fork. Rosalie's nose caught the heavy, enticing aroma of garlic and tomato sauce. She dumped her sandwich back into its bag and picked up the fork, not commenting on suddenly being served by her boss.

Jacob returned to his seat. "In the meantime, however, let's talk about something else."

"That's going to be hard, Jacob. The book is on my mind. What would you like to talk about?" Rosalie asked between bites.

"Unimportant little things that happen to us," Jacob said, a note of excitement in his voice. "Things ordinary people talk about."

Rosalie's heart went out to her author friend. He wanted to learn how to interact. But was she really the one to teach him?

"Jacob, didn't your family talk at the table?"

Jacob chewed carefully and swallowed, dabbing at his mouth with the napkin. He set the napkin back on his knee before continuing.

"When I was little, the dinner table was a place where children were expected to show their manners through silence," he began. "My father often had guests for dinner, and he talked loudly and constantly. Neither my mother nor I said much—my mother because she was withdrawn and didn't care to be there; me, because my father expected it. I was chastised if I let my fork scrap the plate too loud and God forbid that I spill a drop of milk or a bit of food."

Rosalie couldn't imagine how difficult his childhood had been. *My poor Just Jacob,* she thought.

"By the time I was an adult and my mom was gone," Jacob continued, "I had nothing much to say to the man, though later in life, we discussed my books. It felt as if I wasn't even real to him until my name became known."

He was silent for several moments and then took several more bites of lasagna.

"After he died, I was just in the habit of remaining quiet at the dinner table, and I guess I inherited a little of my mom's shyness. I've only had guests a couple of times over the years," he said, a faraway look in his eyes.

His face brightened as he turned to Rosalie. "But I want to talk, I want to leave food on my plate, and I want to let my napkin fall to the floor. Does that make any sense to you?"

Rosalie stopped chewing, but didn't look up from her plate. "Yes, Jacob, it does make sense. Despite the fact that my upbringing was about as far from yours as humanly possible."

"And what was dinner at your table like?" Jacob asked.

Rosalie shook her head and laid her fork down.

"My mother never shut up and she was always trying to get me to talk. She would go on and on about some other parent's kid who was in the school play, or later in life, about some girl getting married. Meanwhile, she cooked these heavy elaborate meals, put the food on the table, and then chastised me as I ate it. I think she thought she was teaching me self-control, but all she did was make me fat and a secret eater."

"Yes. I can see she likes to talk from my brief encounter at your house, Rosie."

Rosalie, startled, looked up from her food to see a small grin on Jacob's face. It disappeared and his face reddened slightly.

"Oh, I'm sorry. I didn't mean to give you a nickname and I certainly meant no disrespect to your mother." The grin returned. "But somehow Rosalie seems too formal. Do you mind if I call you Rosie?"

"No one's ever called me that and you haven't disrespected my mother. She's a chatterbox." She sat back and tilted her head. "Rosie… I kind of like it. And maybe I can call you Jake? Jacob sounds like one of the heroes in your books."

Jacob's smile broadened. "I've never had a nickname before… Rosie." He sat back as well, his plate still half full, but his meal finished. "And I do not understand your reference to your weight." He was staring at her now and Rosalie felt her own face redden.

"In fact, I think you look very… womanly. Round and soft and very pretty." And then it was his turn to feel embarrassed. He rose and grabbed his plate to take to the kitchen. Rosalie, who had lost any desire to eat more, followed him.

In the kitchen they scraped the remaining food into the disposal and then rinsed the dishes at the sink, neither saying a word. Jacob opened the dishwasher, grabbed Rosalie's dish and loaded both on the bottom rack. Rosalie was surprised at his ease with the domestic task. *He must have been taking care of himself like this for many years and not relying on his housekeeper to do it all*, she thought.

Instead of bringing out the big black car for the trip to the mall, Jacob picked up the phone and called a cab. It wasn't far away.

In the cab, Rosalie finally broke the silence. Turning to Jacob she said, "Jake, something has been bothering me. I don't mean to pry, but how did you come to be writing the graphic portions of your novel? I know they are very popular with the women readers, but they don't seem…you don't seem…they don't appear based on…"

"Experience, Rosie? Is that what you're wanting to say?"

Rosalie turned a bright red this time, embarrassed once again by her mouth.

"It's okay, Rosie," Jacob chuckled. "And you're partially right. I'm not that experienced with women, though I'm not completely without skills or knowledge." He picked up her hand and Rosalie felt a small thrill at the contact.

"I wrote my first book when I was fifteen. It was romantic, but had no sex in it. I was only a young boy and hadn't yet had a girlfriend. Malcolm used to visit my father frequently—the two of them knew each other in school.

"On one visit, Malcolm mentioned that he had become a literary agent. I got excited, retrieved my manuscript from the study and asked if Malcolm would read one of my books. My father, who had shown no interest at all in my writing, grabbed the manuscript out of my hands, flipped to the middle and started to read aloud, probably intent on mocking me. But Malcolm appeared to be listening, his head tilted and his face showing he was concentrating on the words. When my father jokingly said he was going to 'throw this trash in the fireplace,' Malcolm actually grabbed his arm and stopped him.

"Malcolm had only good things to say and his attention was like a cool drink of water. No one had acknowledged that I even wrote before. He sat down with me and actually spent the next hour or so going over my story. My father was fascinated. He quieted down and left the room, so Malcolm and I could talk.

"Anyway, that's how Malcolm became my agent."

Rosalie's brow was furrowed.

"Oh, the sex. That was Malcolm's idea, and my father agreed. The books were good, but they both said they would not sell without some sex. So 'dear old Dad' bought some pornography and even paid a woman to give me my first sexual encounter."

Now Rosalie's face reflected shock.

"I know, I know. But the books sold quickly once Malcolm took them in that direction. In the early years, my father would suggest where the sex scenes were needed."

Rosalie's shock was replaced by disgust. "You were fifteen when Malcolm became your agent, for goodness sakes! Your father exploited your youth and introduced you to porn before you even had a chance to experience any romance! It's hard for me to believe a father could be so… so…"

Jacob calmed her by squeezing her hand. "I was stupid, but it was the first time my father had ever acted proud of me. I know, now, it was purely money and fame. I never should have let him rule my life like he did."

"Where was your mother in all this?" Rosalie asked.

"She died when I was just eighteen. Before that, she was usually in bed with the curtains drawn. I don't think she knew anything about what we were doing together, just as she knew nothing about my father's other lady friends. I found out about them soon after she passed away when he started bringing them to the house."

"And when your dad died?" Rosalie asked quietly. It was her turn to squeeze Jacob's hand.

"That was just a decade ago. By that time, the process for putting together a book was so ingrained in me, I just kept writing the same way."

Suddenly, Jacob was angry.

"What I didn't realize is that I had been writing to a formula—at a certain point the girl meets the boy, the boy makes a play, the girl refuses him, and eventually they end up together in bed. I don't think I realized I was no longer telling stories, just writing scenes, until I sat down last night to make a tape without that formula in my head."

The cab had arrived at the mall. Before he reached for payment, Jacob turned to gaze at Rosalie, his hand still holding hers. "Thanks, Rosie. I feel like somehow, you've freed me from my own chains."

Chapter 25

The author and his assistant walked the mall corridors, not saying much of anything for the first forty-five minutes. Jacob felt as if he'd been transported to a different world—one that sparkled from so many sources of light and glitter.

Rosalie saw his amazement and let him soak in the visual stimulation before she finally placed a hand gently on his forearm, suggesting they sit for a time. They'd arrived at the food court, where they spent the next two hours sipping fruit drinks and coffee, all the while making up details about the people they saw. Rosalie brought paper and a pen, and took notes on the stories that erupted from Jacob's thoughts at ever quickening speeds as he sought to stretch his mind.

When at last, Jacob's brain seemed to wind down and Rosalie's writing hand began to ache, the two called a cab and prepared to leave. As they waited for the cab to arrive, Jacob gazed toward a tall fence, a taller Ferris wheel, and the back-end of food trucks. In the park that joined the mall at one end, a carnival was testing rides in preparation for the weekend throngs.

"I went to a fair once," Jacob said, one hand shielding his eyes from the late afternoon sun. Rosalie couldn't read his eyes.

"I think I was probably about seven." His hand dropped and he turned towards the designated cabstand. Rosalie didn't want to let the moment pass. "And how did that happen?"

Jacob turned back to her, a look of surprise on his face, as if he hadn't realized he'd said anything out loud.

The cab arrived and they got in. Jacob resumed his tale.

"Ms. Krimshaw was my nanny at the time. Probably the only nanny I remember well. Certainly, the only one I ever cared much for. I liked her because she shielded me from my father, instead of holding the threat of him over my head."

"Ms. Krimshaw told my father one afternoon that I had a dentist appointment. She took me to a fair instead. I didn't really understand why I was there."

Jacob stared out the window.

"And?" Rosalie prodded.

He turned back to meet her gaze and Rosalie was struck by how blue his eyes were; they burned even brighter from the memory he was sharing.

"And she simply led me around, holding tight to my hand; she realized the unfamiliar sights and sounds might scare me. I was frightened at first, but as long as she was holding my hand, I felt safe enough to explore with my eyes. Eventually, I became so excited by what I was seeing, I begged her to take me on a ride. She was reluctant, but finally relented. Then she took me on another, and another, and even fed me cotton candy. She was spending her own money, I'm sure, so we were only there for a short while; my father would never have approved. The memory is one of my better ones from my childhood."

Jacob had a pleasant look on his face, lost in remembrance of a good moment. Rosalie's eyes were round, filled with the beginnings of tears. She gazed out the other window so he would not see. They rode in silence, both lost in thought.

When they pulled up in front of his home, Jacob surprised Rosalie.

"Rosie, don't you think a fair would be a good place to study people?"

***

The following Sunday was a golden afternoon; Jacob and his assistant returned to the park to study the glitz and crowds of the fair.

Jacob got out of the cab and stood for a moment, awkward and unsure of what to do. Rosalie smiled broadly, tilting her head towards the sky to take in the glorious late summer sunshine and then grabbed his hand. The eighty-degree warm weather held little humidity and a soft breeze blew Rosalie's flowered cotton skirt gently against her legs.

Jacob's thoughts quickly returned to his boyhood and the day long ago with his nanny, as he and Rosalie wandered the thoroughfare, hand in hand.

At first, the kids brushing by his hips unsettled him. They had to sidestep loaded-down parents pushing baby carriages and groups of teens traveling in packs. Most people were completely unaware they were invading Jacob's personal space. The smells of grease and perspiration hung in the air; the noise came from every angle.

Rosalie asked nothing of her friend except his companionship, and soon he began to relax, just as he had as a boy. Instead of groups of people, he started to see individuals—a teen with skin problems smiling shyly at a pretty girl as he handed her a giant panda bear; a father lifting his son high over his head and onto his shoulders, laughing as the boy clapped; a carnival hawker missing most of his teeth looking both bored and resigned.

Rosalie bought a funnel cake and the two found a bench where they sat picking the treat apart, savoring the warm sugary pieces. They laughed at what a mess they became. Rosalie, being a more experienced fair-goer, had packed wet wipes in her purse, and when most of the stickiness was gone, they continued their people game.

"What do you suppose that poor fellow's story is?" Jacob asked, pointing toward the perimeter of the park. A very young boy gazed through the chain link fence from outside the carnival, his fingers gripping the twisted metal rungs. His hand came out of the rungs long enough to wipe his nose on his sleeve.

The couple was too far away to read the expression on the boy's face, or see anything but ragged clothes and a head of messy sand-colored hair. From his size, they could tell he was too young to be without adult supervision.

Rosalie rose, alarmed that the boy might have lost his parents. The moment she did, however, the boy turned and ran. Though the couple knew they were too far away to catch him, or do any good, they instinctively walked toward the fence. By the time they arrived, the child was out of sight.

Jacob turned to Rosalie, the joys of the fair momentarily forgotten.

"I don't know that I could make up a story about that one," he said. "Do you suppose he'll be all right?"

Rosalie smiled. "He's probably running back to his parents." She grabbed Jacob's arm, pulling him gently away from the fence. "Did they have a Ferris wheel at the carnival when you were young?"

The author shielded his eyes long enough to see his companion's face. She was gazing upwards. Jacob turned his eyes to trace the path of her vision and looked up at the very tall structure in the middle of the fair, feeling both fear and excitement.

"I don't really remember, Rosie. Do you want to ride?"

In answer, she pulled his hand, leading him towards the ticket booth.

They were the last to board the Ferris wheel and soon they were locked in their seats, the wind whooshing underneath them as they rose upwards.

At the top, Rosalie reached both arms towards the sky, as if she could catch some of the sunshine. She repeated the gesture six times as the wheel made its revolutions.

Suddenly, the wheel stopped with Rosalie and Jacob at the very top. Rosalie turned to see a white-faced Jacob. She chuckled softly and the author turned to her, confusion on his face.

"You think it's funny that this contraption has broken down with us at the top?"

"No, Jake. They are just letting people off."

Jacob's body went slack with relief and he laughed at himself, grabbing her hand.

"I'm really glad I have an expert in my midst," he joked.

The seat jerked again as the wheel resumed its descent. Without thinking of what he was doing, Jacob put his arm around Rosalie to steady her.

Both were aware how close their bodies were. Their thighs were touching gently, and Jacob put his free hand on the gauzy folds of her skirt. His eyes traveled from the bright colors of her skirt, alighted briefly on her generous bosom and then rose upwards to her lips. Rosalie held her breath.

"You look beautiful today, Rosie, I…" He could find no words to continue.

Rosalie simply leaned in, resting her lips on his. It started as the gentle contact of a light, friendly peck before his arm pulled her in closer. Then they lost themselves in the soft sensation of lips against lips and tongue against tongue. Rosalie's hands found their way to the nape of his neck and she pulled him even closer. Both were shocked when they felt another jerk of the Ferris wheel.

***

The next few minutes were awkward as what had happened between them sunk in. When they reached the bottom, Jacob was the first to disembark. He turned back towards Rosalie and offered his hand. She took it and didn't let go for the remainder of the day.

Chapter 26

At ten on Monday morning, Sam Osborne arrived at Jacob's door for a pre-arranged appointment. Instead of Jacob or Catherine, a pretty woman with shiny dark hair, who Sam guessed to be in her late thirties or early forties, answered the door. She explained that Jacob was waiting in the library.

When they arrived in the room, Sam could see they had been sharing a pot of coffee. The woman settled back on the sofa next to Jacob. Sam sat down on an easy chair.

"I need to talk privately with you, Jacob, about an idea I have regarding the statues." He glanced toward Jacob's companion before settling his questioning eyes on Jacob.

"Whatever you have to say to me, you can say in front of her. Rosalie, er… Rosie, this is Sam Osborne, the detective I told you about. Sam, Rosalie McGovern, my assistant," Jacob said. "She's typing my manuscript and advising me on the content."

Sam noticed she looked surprised at Jacob's words, but she recovered quickly and smiled warmly. *So, this is the young woman that made his client so nervous,* Sam thought.

"Of course, Jacob," Sam said. "Nice to meet you Rosalie." He took out his notebook and flipped it open.

"I noted the dates when the incidents occurred and one factor they have in common is that they occur on nights with clear weather, most likely, a few hours after you retire.

"I now know the probable point of entry—the doggie door Catherine and I uncovered—and I believe the best way to catch the thief is to be here the next time he strikes."

"Whatever you feel is best," Jacob said. His mind didn't seem to be on his words.

"You don't sound too convinced," Sam said. His eyes rose from his notes to settle again on the couple. Jacob's attention was on Rosalie, who was listening to Sam's words. She glanced at Jacob, smiled again and took a sip of coffee.

Jacob turned toward Sam. "Oh, I am serious, Sam. It makes me angry that someone is invading my home and taking my possessions. It's just not the priority it once was."

"But I assume you'd like me to continue this investigation?" Sam asked.

"Yes, of course, Sam. You're the professional. I value your opinion and direction." Jacob sat up straighter in his chair as if to give Sam's words more attention. Sam's eyes returned to his notes.

"You said the thief comes in fair weather and the doggie door may be the point of entry?" Jacob prodded.

"I believe he picks dry nights so that no footprints or muddy tracks are left. That doggie door is the only vulnerable point in the house and it looks like someone has tampered with it."

The author's head cocked slightly at Sam's words.

"The funny thing is, I don't remember Mother's dog," Jacob said.

"Catherine told me about Buttons. Apparently, the dog disappeared a few years after you were born so you wouldn't remember it. The door was built to let the dog out and it's almost invisible from this side and situated behind some grown bushes on the outside. It was nailed shut at one point, but I can see that someone has loosened the boarding enough to use it, with a little effort."

Now Jacob was leaning slightly forward, his interest piqued. "A little effort?"

"I'm puzzled, Jacob, because the door is tiny. It has to be a very small child, a midget with skills at maneuverability, or a trained animal to get through the door."

Jacob glanced at Rosalie and then back at Sam, his eyebrows raised in inquiry.

"And what is your theory as to who might be squeezing through this contraption?" he asked.

"I don't know, Jacob. And I don't know how all this is connected to what I've been investigating, as far as the statues themselves and where they're going—I've made some progress on that end. But that door is the only way I can see that someone could be gaining access."

Sam made sure he had both Rosalie's and Jacob's full attention.

"I want to set up a sting in the next night or so, if your schedule permits. I really don't believe the thief can be dangerous—he's too small. I'll have backup ready to go anyway, in case we need it."

Rosalie finally spoke.

"You think the easiest way to find out who the thief is, is to catch him red handed?"

"Exactly, Ms. McGovern," Sam said.

"Rosalie or Rosie, please, Sam," she said.

Sam's eyes traveled from her calm gentle smile to Jacob's still puzzled face.

"So are you two up for this?" the detective asked. "The sun on Sunday dried the ground and the sunny weather is supposed to stick around for the next few days. I have a meeting with someone in Harrisburg Wednesday, but we could try it tonight, or tomorrow night."

The two exchanged a glance and Sam felt that pull between two people that is sometimes visible in couples that have been together for awhile. They even nodded in unison and Sam realized that Jacob had not even questioned Sam's inclusion of Rosalie in the sting.

Hmmm, Sam thought. *They got to know each*

other pretty quickly.

"We may as well do this as soon as possible," Jacob said. He turned back toward the detective. "I imagine someone has to be watching the house enough to know I go to bed at about eleven. If you'll hide your car early this evening, Sam, I think we can fool that someone. I'll let you in the back way. Rosalie can just stay here today after work." His eyes returned to his assistant. "That is, if you're available, Rosie."

"Of course, Jake," she said and Sam noted the author now had a nickname.

Jacob rose from the sofa and extended his hand towards Sam. "If you can come around seven, I'll have Catherine leave us some dinner and we can wait out the burglar."

"I'll see you at seven this evening then," Sam said. They shook hands and the detective left the author and his assistant to their day's work.

He was smiling as he got into his car.

Good for you, Jake. Good for you.

Chapter 27

Mr. Sir reached down, took ahold of the blankets covering the little boy and jerked. "Get up, lazy boy," his gruff voice commanded. "You've been sleeping all day. You've got a big job in a few hours."

Wretched groaned and sat up. His skin felt like it was on fire and every bone in his body ached. "I don't feel so good," he whimpered, trying to keep from tumbling back onto his bed. He wished the image of Mr. Sir would stand still.

"Nonsense, boy. You can't be sick. Tonight is extremely important. I'm going on vacation after this job is done and you, my boy, will be rich if you can carry this off. See how I've changed your carrying sling so that it can hold three tied back to back? Three statues, boy. That's nine dollars and I'm giving you a bonus, so ten dollars!"

"I don't feel so good," Wretched repeated, his voice hoarse from his scratchy throat.

Mr. Sir crossed his arms and scowled at the boy. He reached into his pocket and drew out a small bottle. "I brought you some magic medicine, Wretched. Take it, and your throat will feel all better. Take it, and your head won't hurt."

"But my arm hurts bad, too," the boy cried, holding a swollen limb out to the man.

Mr. Sir reached in his other pocket and brought out a tube of ointment.

"This will help the arm, boy. It will make the scratch stop hurting." Mr. Sir reached for the boy's arm, but when he touched it, Wretched screamed and drew away.

Mr. Sir took a step back to avoid the flailing arm. He scowled again, leaning forward. Instead of touching the boy, he scooped up the tiny cat that lay on the boy's pillow.

Wretched's face contorted with his pain and now, an added anxiety.

Mr. Sir, however, had grown quite calm. His voice was deeper than Wretched had ever heard it.

"You will do as I say, or I'll wring this damn pest's neck."

Mr. Sir took the cat by the scruff of the neck and waved it in front of Wretched's face. With his other hand, he picked up the bottle of medicine and slammed it down on the bed.

"You will take your medicine and finish this work, or you will not have a cat any longer," Mr. Sir said through clenched teeth.

He tossed the kitten on the bed beside the boy, went over to the faucet, and filled one of the small paper cups with water. He took the water back to the boy, dug a pill out of the bottle he brought, and held both out to Wretched.

"Take this," Mr. Sir said, his voice now soothing. "Soon you'll be better, you will be ten dollars richer and you can buy yourself something very special at the mall."

He laid the paper cup and pills on the cardboard box that served as Wretched's nightstand, and then reached for the tube of salve on the bed to spread some on his fingers. He held his hand over the boy's red arm and softly said, "You see, Mr. Sir always takes care of you, boy. He only asks that you take care of him. I know that you don't feel good, but this is very important to me. More important than anything I've asked you to do so far. This job has to be done tonight. All you have to do is take the pills and do the excellent work that you always do."

The boy, hungry for kindness, responded to Mr. Sir's gentler voice by relaxing. He didn't flinch much when Mr. Sir rubbed the salve on his arm and when the man was finished, the boy reached for the pills and water.

"Okay," Wretched said. "I'll try very hard, Mr. Sir. I don't want to mess up, but my arm hurts pretty bad."

In the same gentle voice, Mr. Sir added, "Do it right—or the kitten will be gone when you return, Wretched. Do you understand me, boy?"

"Yes," Wretched said, his voice trembling a bit. "I understand."

Mr. Sir left the room.

Wretched looked under the bed where the kitten had fled and drew out his only friend and then sat holding the small kitten close to his body with his eyes closed. He knew he could not sleep. He had only a few hours to rest before it was time for him to do the most important job he had ever done. Once it was done, he might have enough money to be free.

Chapter 28

At seven on Monday night, Sam arrived at Jacob's house and parked several blocks away. Sam, Rosalie, and Jacob enjoyed the rosemary-scented pot roast that Mrs. Wells had left and then sat sipping coffee, getting caught up.

Jacob shared with Sam the new direction his book was taking, while Rosalie interjected with comments about how it was going.

Sam filled the couple in on what he'd found out about the thefts.

"The statues that have gone missing from your home, Jacob, are ending up in the hands of a wealthy collector in Harrisburg, Pennsylvania by the name of Laughlin Cosby. I'm looking into his connections and whether he is a legitimate buyer. I'll be talking to a friend of mine in the Harrisburg police department on Wednesday and they'll help with the investigation and follow-up, if we find out he knew the statues were stolen."

After coffee, the three retired to the living room to await the late hours.

Jacob and Rosalie sat on the couch side by side. At one point, Jacob put his arm around Rosalie. Sam saw her stiffen for just a brief moment and glance over in his direction. But she relaxed quickly and leaned back against Jacob's arm.

"Do you really think the thief will strike tonight?" Rosalie asked softly.

"Yes, I do," Sam answered. "The thefts appear to be happening more frequently. My instincts tell me the thief has given into greed and the fact he has a buyer, or middleman, gives him confidence. He or she probably knows we are getting close to figuring this out, too. I think he'll go for a major theft, if not tonight, then over the course of the next day or so."

"Any thoughts on who it might be?" Jacob asked. The author didn't sound angry or even concerned, just curious.

"Not yet. I had the blood I found on one of the nails sent to a lab today. We won't know the exact results for awhile, but the lab did share that it was human, not animal. If the person responsible for the thefts is in a database, we may get lucky and get a match. However, I don't think the person fitting through that hole is likely to be a local. It's either a midget with maneuverability skills, or a child."

"But what does a child want with Jake's statues? And who told the thief the statues were there?" Rosalie asked.

"That's key here, Rosalie," Sam said. "Someone knew about how valuable they were. He or she also knows Jacob's schedule. There has to be someone close to you who started all of this. I wondered about Kevin Wells, since the thefts started the day he got out of prison. I have no idea, however, how he could have planned it in such a short time without help from Mrs. Wells. And I'm having difficulty seeing her as a culprit unless she is a really fine actress. She also led me to that doggie door, which I don't think she would have done if she knew what was going on."

Sam then turned to Jacob. "Jacob, I want to ask: have you signed anything that would give Malcolm permission to make movies from your books?"

Jacob raised his eyebrows, clearly taken aback. "I wouldn't do that. I have no reason to want my books made into movies. No, I am sure I never gave him such permission. Why?"

"My secretary Casey has looked into this and we believe that he is taking your basic plots, spicing them up and making adult movies out of them. Proving that would be up to a prosecutor in a court of law, but I found out enough to know that your characters are showing up in pornographic films that loosely follow your plots."

Jacob rose, clearly angry. He began to pace in front of the couch.

"There's more," Sam added. Jacob stopped in mid-stride and turned towards Sam.

"Casey looked into a lot of people's past records and we found out your agent has one. It's been a few years, but the man served time twice—once for theft from an apparent con job and once for embezzlement from a company he worked with for a short time in his early thirties."

"So do you think he's mixed up in this theft?" Rosalie asked.

"I can't make a direct connection until I find

out who's doing the buying, but I don't understand what his reasoning would be for taking the statues. Adult movie making and publishing are much more lucrative than stealing a few statues," Sam said.

Jacob returned to his spot beside Rosalie on the couch, and the three sat in silence for a few minutes lost in their thoughts.

Sam interrupted the reverie. "Jacob, did you know that Malcolm, Kevin Wells and Horace Montgomery went to school with your father?"

"Of course. As I explained, I made my initial contact with Malcolm through my father. They remained close and I've known Kevin most of my life, so I know his background. When I was young and he was the gardener, I used to hang around him, watching him work on the grounds. He was quite good with the flowers and plants. When Kevin was convicted, dad hired Horace to do the job and explained that he, too, was a classmate, though I don't think they knew each other that well in school."

Jacob was on his feet again.

"As far as Kevin and Catherine, Sam, I just don't believe it. Catherine has always been very good to me. So good in fact that, well, I helped her come up with the new lawyer that finally proved Kevin's innocence."

Rosalie reached for Jacob's hand as he passed by her end of the couch and pulled him back down beside her. She smiled and raised a hand to brush a lock of hair back from his forehead.

Jacob turned to Sam. "I cannot believe the Wells' would pay me back that way, though I'm not sure Catherine ever told Kevin I hired that lawyer."

"I don't know anything yet and I haven't found out much about Horace," Sam said. "But those two and Catherine are closest to this house and would know your whereabouts and comings and goings. Even if we catch the thief red-handed tonight, we may not have the actual person profiting from the statues. But we'll be much closer."

***

Around eleven, Jacob rose from his spot on the couch and began turning off lights in the same sequence he always used before turning in.

For the next two-and-a-half hours, the three sat in near silence, occasionally whispering. The only real light in the room was Sam's cell phone screen as he texted and made a couple of calls, including one to ensure the police backup was in place. Eventually, Sam rested his head against the back of the chair and allowed himself to close his eyes and rest.

He could hear rustling in the general direction of Rosalie and Jacob and thought he heard the sound of kissing, a sound that created a surprising longing.

It had been way too long since Sam had experienced what the two of them were going through.

Tick, tick, tick.

Suddenly, Sam's head jerked forward. He must

have fallen asleep.

He could sense that the author and his assistant were also sitting up, alert to the sounds coming from the kitchen.

A soft patter of feet moved in their direction. Someone was on the way from the kitchen to the statue room.

Sam reached towards the lamp he had placed close to his chair and turned on the light. The thief was only a few feet away and Sam was on his feet in an instant.

***

Wretched couldn't see anything—the light was too bright. Someone grabbed his arm and a scream escaped his lips.

"You hurt him!" a woman's voice cried.

"No, I barely touched him. Something is wrong with his arm..."

Wretched was lying on the floor. *How did I get on the floor?*

"He's so small! My God, he's burning up!"

The room was getting dark again as Wretched fought to keep his eyes open. His arm was on fire; his throat was on fire. He struggled to sit, but fell back down.

***

The next time he opened his eyes, Wretched

was in a moving vehicle. Looking down at him was an angel. Her soft shiny black hair encircled her head, but he saw kindness in her eyes. His head rested in the soft folds of her dress. Her hand held his firmly. "You'll be okay," she whispered. "We're almost there."

"Am I dead? Are you taking me to visit God?" the little boy whispered in awe.

"No," the angel told him. "To the hospital."

Wretched closed his eyes again. He didn't care where he was going. He wondered if the angel was his mother. She was comfortable and gentle and she smelled like flowers. Suddenly, the boy was no longer afraid of anything. He went to sleep with a smile on his face.

Chapter 29

When Wretched opened his eyes, he saw a man with the angel sitting beside him on the bed, holding hands. He recognized the angel from the car ride, but who was the man? Their faces looked tired and their eyes sleepy; they gazed at him with worry.

"Am I in heaven?" he asked the angel again. "Will I get to see God now?" His throat hurt a lot and his words sounded scratchy.

The woman rose out of her chair and came to sit on the bed beside him.

"You're not dead, dear," the woman said in a soft voice. She chuckled and swept his hair back from his forehead. Wretched was not used to such contact, but it felt good.

"I was very hot, then very cold," Wretched said. He looked from one side of the room to the next. "Where am I?"

"You're in the hospital," the woman said. "You've been quite sick, little one. You had a very bad cold—almost pneumonia, the doctor said. And your arm was infected. You were hot and cold because you had a high temperature. But you feel better now, right?"

The man came to stand close to the angel woman.

"You almost lost your arm, young man," he said.

Alarmed, Wretched glanced down at the big bandage on his arm. He moved it to reassure himself that it still worked and then noticed how clean it was, as was his other arm.

"Am I clean all over?" he asked.

Before Rosalie or Jacob could answer, however, Wretched yawned, closed his eyes and fell asleep again.

***

Rosalie and Jacob both sighed. They were relieved that the boy woke up, if only for a short time. He was so tiny and skinny. Even though they had known the thief was someone very small, they were shocked that this thin child had been the culprit.

His clothes, which the doctors had replaced with a clean hospital gown, had hung on his bony frame. They were so ragged that the staff had thrown them away. The poor boy's body was covered with a layer of mud and dirt thick enough that the staff weren't sure of his ethnicity until they gave him a cleaning.

Rosalie smiled as she remembered the boy's brief awakening in the ambulance. He had believed she was an angel and for some reason it pleased her, but not nearly as much as when Jake had whispered, "You have that right, little one! She's our own special angel."

None of the three—she, Jake or Sam Osborne—had hesitated in coming to the small thief's aid. The boy was obviously in pain and had fainted when Sam grabbed him. Luckily, it had taken just five minutes for the EMS to reach Jacob's home.

Social Services and the police had been called, but neither Rosalie nor Jacob could bring themselves to leave the small boy by himself there in the hospital. He was lost in the big bed; his body now clean from the wash, his breathing soft and steady as he slept. Rosalie and Jacob held hands through the long night, agreeing without discussing, to stay by the boy's side.

"He is so little," Rosalie whispered to Jacob, for what had to be the hundredth time in the last six hours. Jacob's arm was around her as they sat in hospital chairs. She snuggled closer and laid her head on his shoulder. "I wonder who he is and where he lives."

"I don't know," Jacob replied, "But I'd like to find the sadistic person who made him climb through that door and steal the statues. I'm sure it wasn't the child's idea—and he obviously hasn't profited from the thefts."

"And we thought we had it rough growing up!" Rosalie exclaimed.

"At least we always had someone watching over us, keeping us safe and fed. Our woes look pretty pitiful next to this child, don't they?"

"Yes. No matter how annoying my mom can get, I always knew she cared for me. I don't think this little kid has had anyone watching over him for a long while."

Wretched opened his eyes again.

"I'm thirsty," he croaked. Rosalie put a small ice chip in his mouth. He smiled his thanks and was fast asleep again.

***

After visiting briefly with a woman from Social Services to fill her in on what had happened, as well as a police officer who stopped by to fill out an official report, Rosalie and Jacob knew they needed to go home. Nothing would be decided about the boy until he was feeling better.

The couple was exhausted; every bone in their bodies felt the all-nighter they'd pulled. Jacob dropped Rosalie off at her house and then went to his own home for a shower and sleep.

As agreed, the two were back at the hospital by evening visiting hours. They were surprised and delighted to see the little boy sitting up with a tray of food in front of him. Although the doctor had put him on a bland diet, he acted as if it was a gourmet meal. He ate heartily of the applesauce and mashed potatoes and then savored the wiggling Jell-O, keeping each bite in his mouth for a while before swallowing.

When he looked up from one of those bites and saw Jacob and Rosalie, a huge smile lit his face. "I am eatin'," he declared. "And it ain't cereal!"

Jacob and Rosalie laughed, caught up in the child's enthusiasm. They sat down in chairs beside the bed. They were holding hands again and feeling happy that the youngster was out of danger.

"What is your name, boy?" Jacob asked.

"Don't know," the boy replied, his concentration again on the food. "Mr. Sir calls me Wretched."

"Mr. Sir?" Jacob asked. "Is that a friend?"

The boy shook his head and took another bite of Jell-O. "Nah. He's my boss. Brings me cereal for my tummy and pays me two dollars if I do a job right!"

"He pays you to take stuff out of people's houses?" Jacob kept his voice steady as he asked the question, not wanting to alarm the child.

Wretched was too smart for that. He stopped eating completely and a look of fear crossed his features. The beautiful smile was gone.

"Are you the cops?" he asked slowly, his eyes avoiding theirs.

"Oh, no," Rosalie assured him, reaching over to pat his shoulder. "We are just friends."

"Friends?" the little boy questioned, finally looking up. His eyes narrowed. "I ain't got no friends. You was in the house last night! Are you going to haul me off to jail?"

Sam Osborne came into the room in time to hear the boy's last words. The detective smiled when the boy looked over at him.

"Hello, there," Sam said, his tone friendly. "These nice people are not the police. I'm not the police either. I'm a private detective. Do you know what that is?"

Wretched shook his head, his eyes still fearful.

"I look into mysteries," Sam continued. "Doesn't that sound like fun?"

The boy's head nodded up and down slowly and curiosity began to replace the fear.

"The statues disappearing out of that house have been a big mystery to me," Sam continued. "For a long time, I wondered how someone could get into a locked house. I never thought of the doggy door. That was very clever of you."

"Not me. Mr. Sir is the clever one. He jes' hired me 'cause I'm small. That was my job," the boy answered, a tinge of pride creeping into his voice.

"And you apparently did it well. But how did you scratch your arm?"

"I knowed that nail was on the door. I guess I wasn't paying attention 'cause of my cold. It hurt somethin' awful, but I didn't cry." He pushed the table tray out and leaned back against the pillow, pulling the covers up to his chin.

"I saw your special carrying sack. It was pretty big. Were you going to take the rest of the statues?" Sam asked.

"Naw. I cain't carry that many. But Mr. Sir said I was to take at least three. And he was going to pay me ten dollars! That was enough for…" The boy looked around at all three adults and shut his mouth. He scrunched back against the comfy pillow and shut his eyes.

Sam took the hint and decided to leave the boy in peace. He could resume his questioning when the child was feeling more comfortable. Just now, the boy appeared to either fall asleep or be very good at acting. Sam motioned for Jacob and Rosalie to follow him into the hall.

"I'm going to resume my investigation tomorrow and will be driving to Harrisburg later in the day. I'll probably be back late tomorrow night, or the next morning. I need to follow up on a lead I got late last week and talk to the police department. I'll let you know what I find out when I return. Take good care of our young thief. He could use some friends until Social Services have a chance to take care of him and we can find out who he is."

The couple nodded and said, almost in unison, "We'll take care of him."

Chapter 30

Sam's determination to find the person responsible for the thefts ratcheted up several degrees with the realization that someone had coached a tiny boy in how to become a thief and then hadn't cared for his or her protégé properly when the boy was hurt. The detective was certain the little guy would tell them what he could. However, Sam wasn't sure the boy knew enough to help them find and prosecute the person profiting from the sales of the statues.

After coffee and a quick discussion with his assistant Casey, the detective decided to stick with his original intent for the day, which was to feel around for more details on Kevin Wells and Horace Montgomery, and then travel to Harrisburg to track down more information on where the statues were going.

He arrived at the Wells' home just before noon and approached this time from the front, instead of the mansion's side yard. No one answered the doorbell or his loud knocking, but Sam could hear music playing.

After several minutes, Catherine Wells came to the door, her hands covered with a dusting of flour. She nudged the door open with a knee and foot. "Come in, Sam, come in. If you want to talk, you'll have to follow me to the kitchen."

As they walked to the kitchen, Sam complemented the housekeeper/cook on the meal he'd enjoyed Monday night, letting his eyes wander around the rest of the home. The detective decided the house fit Catherine's personality. Like her kitchen, the rest of the home was warm and inviting, highlighted with splashes of color from knick-knacks, curtains, and pillows. None of it looked high price. The effect was cozy, and Sam felt right at home.

"I didn't get much of a chance to talk to your husband when I was at the house the day we discovered the door, Catherine. Is he here?" Sam asked.

"Kevin's outside—in our backyard." Catherine nodded towards the back window. "He's busy with yard work, but I think he'd welcome the interruption. He's busy hoeing weeds. Here, take him this iced tea." She reached for a glass and filled it with cold, sweet liquid.

Sam found Kevin where Catherine had indicated and the man seemed friendlier, or at least more relaxed than last time, especially after Sam handed him the cold drink. He smiled and indicated a bench, where the two sat. Kevin sipped his tea slowly as Sam asked about his former school friends.

"Yes, we were all pretty good buddies at one time—at least Oswald, Malcolm and me. We were the same age. I guess we were troublemakers in our own way. Got into a few scrapes with the school officials for the pranks we played. That was a long time ago, though. What's that got to do with anything now?" Kevin took out a handkerchief and wiped his forehead.

"I was just wondering if you'd remained friends over the years?" Sam asked. "I know a lot has happened since those days."

Kevin suddenly reverted to the man with ruffled-feathers that Sam had first encountered. "Yeah, you could definitely say a lot has happened! The changes started a long time before my arrest, however. Things were real different after we graduated and Oswald landed himself a wife richer than his own family. I guess he saw it as a big step up in the world. He'd already decided we were no longer worth hanging out with. By the time I became his gardener, I hadn't had much to do with him for years. I did appreciate the job, but I certainly did not fraternize with the boss."

Kevin then seemed to make an effort to lose the anger. He stood up from the bench, stretched, and sat back down, taking a long draw from his tea. His expression turned reflective again and Sam drew out his pen and paper to take notes.

"I didn't mind being his gardener, really. It paid very well. However, I have to admit I was taken aback when Oswald not only fired me, but started acting liked he'd never known me after the arrest. He wouldn't even testify as a character witness at my trial."

Sadness touched Kevin's features. "And he wasn't the only one. Almost all of our so-called friends forgot about me when I went to jail." Kevin wiped his forehead again and put the cloth in his breast pocket. He shook his head back and forth slowly and looked straight at Sam.

"You know, marrying money may have moved Oswald up the social ladder, but I'd take my woman over that useless wimp Millie Foxe any day. Catherine stood by me every minute I was in prison. She was the only person who knew I wouldn't steal a nickel—she was the only one who believed an innocent man had gone to jail. No, I never heard a word from anyone those years I was in jail."

Even though Sam knew the answer to the next question, he wanted to draw Kevin Wells out, to try to see how deep the bitterness about his false conviction went.

"How did you get out after just three-and-a-half years, Mr. Wells?"

Kevin's face brightened immediately. "DNA and a new lawyer Catherine found for me—one that believed in my innocence, just like she always did. I am lucky to have had such a woman—steadfast and true—that's my Catherine."

"And did they ever find the true thief?" Sam continued.

"No. The damn police spent a lot of time just trying to pin it on me. And even with the fancy new DNA testing the lawyer got done, they couldn't find someone to match up with the crime."

Sam looked up from his note taking. "And how about the rest of the boys from high school? Did you remain friends with any of them over the years?"

"Naw, not at all. I guess old Oswald was the glue for our gang in school. He gave the gardener's job to Horace after I was put away, so I see that guy around here, of course. We hung out together once in a while before jail happened, but I never was that friendly with him, even back in school. Horace tried to hang out with Oswald, Malcolm, and me in school, but he was always the low man on the totem pole. Kind of the follower-type—hung on every word Oswald uttered."

"And Malcolm?"

Kevin thought for a moment before replying.

"Oswald was the boss of our group, and I guess Malcolm was his trusty second in command. I see old Malcolm hobbling into the house once in awhile to see the author, but hell, I have no reason to give him the time of day. Oswald was sometimes downright mean. And Malcolm was a crook! The only reason he got through high school in the first place was he learned to steal tests and sell the answers. No, I got no use for him or Horace anymore."

Sam changed the subject. "Didn't you tell me you'd seen these statues that have disappeared? Could you elaborate on when that was?" Sam's pen was poised over his notebook.

"Catherine told me about those things while I was in prison. Told me how fascinated the author was with them. I was curious what the fuss was about, so when I got home, she let me into the room for a quick look. Seemed like a shelf of junk to me, Mr. Osborne. Nothin' very attractive about 'em, to my way of thinking. Hard to understand how a man could think so much of those statues. They all look pretty much the same."

Then Kevin threw back his shoulders and sat a little taller. "I swear that's the only time I ever saw those things! I like Jacob—he's certainly much nicer than his old dad and even nicer now that Oswald's gone. I would never take something of Jacob's."

"Understood, Kevin." Sam stood up. He wondered why Kevin didn't mention the financial support from Jacob that had earned his freedom. Was it possible Catherine had not told her husband that Jacob had picked up the legal bill?

Sam shook Kevin's hand, thanked him for his time and asked if he'd seen Horace on the grounds that day.

"I don't think so," Kevin said. "Haven't seen him in a few days. I haven't told Catherine this yet, but Mr. Hardy mentioned giving me back my job, so I've kind of been starting to get caught up on the yard. Horace never was too good at it."

"Jacob is firing Horace?" Sam asked, surprised that he was just now finding this out.

"Oh, no. He would never do such a thing. Jacob ain't like his old man. He just said I was better with plants and keeping up with things than Horace. I think Jacob will keep Horace around. He's kind of a handyman, apparently and has a side business fixing things. Jacob just said he'd let Horace do some of his driving and maybe some of the work that needs done inside the house, but that I could take up most of the outside work."

Sam congratulated Kevin on the possibility of having the caretaker job back and the two men shook hands. Sam decided he'd get Horace's side business phone number from Casey and call to set up an appointment. He'd stop at the hospital for a brief interview with the boy and then drive to Harrisburg to find out more about where the statues were going.

Chapter 31

Jacob and Rosalie watched the boy as he slept. They did not speak. They did not touch, except to hold hands. The quietness in the room was a thread that sewed their similar thoughts together. Both were trying to visualize a way to help the small boy in the bed. Neither had come up with a specific plan, they just felt a mutual pull towards the boy.

Suddenly, Jacob turned toward Rosalie and grasped her hand tighter.

"I want to thank you," he said, his voice soft so that he didn't wake the lad.

Rosalie's brows rose. "For what?" she whispered.

"I'm sitting here visualizing something I never thought I'd even think about, Rosie."

Rosalie tilted her head in question.

"I want to help this boy. I want to find out who he is and see if there's some way I can assure he never has to be a thief again."

"Jacob, that's wonderful. What are you thanking me for?"

"I'm not exactly sure how you've done this. You've made me a different person."

"Jake, darling, you're the same man you've always been. You're just looking at things differently."

Jacob felt his blood warm when she used the word "darling." *Did she know what she'd just said?*

Rosalie un-knitted their hands and reached up to outline his face. She loved how sharp his features were, yet how young he looked for forty-six. *Well, heck, he was young in many ways and fairly naïve, yet so masculine.* She loved how deeply blue his eyes were, especially when he was lost in thought.

"Jake, you've done far more for me than I've done for you."

It was Jacob's turn to look confused.

"In just the short time I've known you, you've managed to wipe out many years of having my mother tell me how fat and unattractive I was. You've brought out self-confidence I did not know I possessed. So thank you, darling."

This time he knew he'd heard her right, and he knew she realized what she was saying.

He put his hands up on both sides of her head and brought her face and lips closer to his. The kiss they shared this time was not innocent in any way. It continued for several minutes, growing more blinding as their feelings emerged.

A small giggle from the bed startled the lovers, who pulled back suddenly, breathing deeply to calm themselves.

"Is you guys married folk?" the little boy

asked.

Jacob looked from Wretched to Rosalie and saw her bemused smile. The couple settled back against their seats and resumed holding hands.

"Perhaps we will be one day, young man. But that's none of your business at the moment."

The little boy's face fell at Jacob's words. "I'm sorry, mister. I didn't mean no disrespect."

"Relax, lad. No offense taken." Jacob smiled broadly to reassure the boy and changed the subject. "So what do they call you besides Wretched, son?"

The boy brought his hand to his chin and rubbed as if he was puzzled by the question.

"That's all I got fer a name."

"But what did your mother and father call you?" Jacob asked

"I don't know. I don't think I had no mother or father. Mr. Sir takes care of me," the boy answered, the look on his face growing more confused.

"Are you an orphan, then?" Rosaline inquired. "Did you live in a foster home, perhaps?" She knew they needed information if they were to find out more about the child.

At her words, Wretched grabbed his covers and pulled them up to his chin.

"I didn't like them foster people. They was mean. I ran away. Mr. Sir rescued me." The boy began to look from Rosalie to Jacob, panic starting to form in his eyes. "I need to get home to my kitty, Tiger. I need to get home before Mr. Sir knows I'm gone!"

Seeing his distress, Rosalie retreated from her line of questioning and tried a different approach. She tilted her head. "If you could have any name in the world, what one would you choose?"

That brought a grin from the boy; he released the covers and looked up at the ceiling. After a few moments, his head came back down, and he announced, "Luke. I like Luke."

"Why do you like Luke? Did you know someone named Luke?" Jacob prodded.

"Yeah, I did. Once some big boys were beatin' up on me and this other boy, Luke, made 'em leave me alone. He took care of me for that day and the next, and we was real buddies."

The boy's smile fell.

"Until the cops got him. Then I didn't see him no more. But I still think about him. I liked Luke."

"Well, hello then, Luke," Jacob said, and he shook the boy's hand as if they were just meeting. "I'm Jake and this is Rosie."

The boy giggled, delighted to be a part of grown-up introductions.

Rosalie decided it was a good time to bring up an idea she and Jacob had discussed. "The doctor says you can probably go home tomorrow, or maybe the day after. Instead of going back to Mr. Sir, would you like to come home to Jacob's big house—the house where we found you?"

The boy grabbed his covers again and pulled them over his head.

"No, no, no," Jacob and Rosalie heard from underneath the blankets.

Jacob leaned forward and pulled at the covers on the boy's head. The little boy was holding them tight.

"Calm down, Luke," Jacob said. "What on earth is wrong?"

"I can't go to that house. Please don't make me!" the muffled voice exclaimed.

Rosalie and Jacob exchanged a glance.

"Why, Luke?" Jacob asked. "Why can't you go to the house?"

"Because if he sees me there, he'll kill me," the little boy answered. "Then he'll go home and kill Tiger!"

"Who will kill you, Luke?" Rosalie asked. "Does Mr. Sir live near Jacob's house?"

Luke uncovered his head, but his panic continued.

"I didn't get the things he wanted. He said if I didn't get them, he'd cut me and my cat in little pieces and feed us to the bears!"

"No one is feeding anyone to the bears," Jacob

said, his voice now stern. "If Mr. Sir is taking care of you, boy, why are you afraid of him?"

The little boy didn't know what to say to the question. Suddenly, his eyes filled with tears, which started to spill over.

"He jes' gets mad sometimes," the boy began to whimper. "He's my boss and when I mess up, he doesn't like it. I ain't ever messed up nearly as bad as this…" The whimpers deepened into sobs.

Rosalie got up from her chair and sat down on the bed beside the child. Without thinking about what she was doing, she drew the little body into her arms. Luke stiffened at her touch, but relaxed into her when she began to rub his back.

"Luke, boy. We'll keep you safe," she whispered. "He won't be able to get to you."

The boy was crying so hard now, he was gasping for breath between sobs.

"We'll lock all the doors," Jacob assured him, "and the windows. He can't get through the doggy door. And we have Sam, the man who was with us last night and helped us bring you to the doctor's. Sam will stop him. We'll all stop him."

"He'll send the bear into the house to get to me. I ain't safe in that house."

"Think, boy," Jacob said softly. "The door is so small you could barely get through it—certainly no bear can. Besides, I'll nail it shut. We'll keep you safe."

"He'll get to me, he promised," the boy said, his sobs back to quiet whimpers. "He always does the things he promises."

"We keep our promises, too, Luke. And I promise we'll protect you," Rosalie said.

She held him against her bosom for a few more moments, and then laid the exhausted child, his tears spent, back against the bedclothes. The little boy turned his head to the side, sighed deeply, and went to sleep.

Rosalie and Jacob whispered softly to each other. Rosalie had decided to stay with the boy and then go home to her mother's place in a few hours. She took Luke's hand in hers. Jacob kissed her cheek and left. He drove to his home, went immediately to the caretaker's garage, got out lumber, nails and a hammer, and nailed the doggie door shut – from both inside and outside. Phoning Mrs. Wells, he explained that a guest would be staying and asked her to make up a bed and prepare a special supper for the next day. Then he went upstairs, took a shower, and dropped onto his bed.

"We'll keep you safe, little one," Jacob said out loud. He was very tired, but his mind wouldn't allow him to fall asleep. He was planning what he would do for the boy. His sleeplessness was for naught, though. The problem of how to keep the lad safe was no longer in his or Rosalie's hands.

Chapter 32

"But I thought he was to go home with Mr. Hardy," the nurse said, a worried look on her face.

The social worker shook her gray hair and crossed her arms over her bosom.

"No," she said sternly. "Child Services does not allow a youngster to go home with a perfect stranger. You should know that." She tapped her foot against the floor impatiently as she took identification out of the bag slung over her shoulder and showed the befuddled nurse, then sighed and looked to the ceiling before settling her narrowed eyes on the nurse's face.

"The boy is to be released into my care," she said slowly, enunciating her words. "He will be placed in a foster home until we can decide what to do with him. If Mr. Hardy wants to sponsor him, he has to deal with our office and go through the proper authorities to prove he will make a proper foster parent. For now, the boy comes with me. The doctor has checked him out and into my care."

Luke had been awake ever since the nurse and woman had come into the room. He had pretended to stay asleep to listen to their argument. He opened one eye to peek at the gray-haired woman, who didn't appear to notice. He listened to them with his eyes shut for a few minutes. He knew the lady would win the argument. Although Rosie had promised she'd be here when he awoke, it hadn't happened, and Luke knew going home with the nice Rosie and Jake was not going to happen either. It was too good to be true. He was on his own again. He would have to go with this lady and there would be no more kisses or hugs from the sweet smelling Rosie or handshakes with the handsome man.

At least Mr. Sir might not find me if I go with her, he thought, but the thought gave him no comfort. He wouldn't have Tiger. Luke sighed deeply and opened his eyes. The nurse heard him and turned her attention from the social worker. She explained quietly that the social worker was there to take care of him and that the doctor had said he was okay to leave.

Luke let the nurse help him dress, handling his sore arm gently. The hospital staff had donated a pair of pants and a shirt. Luke took no pride in his new clothes.

When he was dressed, the nurse helped him into a wheelchair, and when she turned her back, the social worker took over. She whisked the boy out of the room and started down the hall. The nurse ran after her. The social worker might know county procedures, but the nurse knew it was the hospital's responsibility to see the child exited the building safely. Shoving the social worker aside, she took over, and just before she helped him into the car, she leaned over and planted a kiss on the boy's cheek. "It will be all right," she whispered. "I'll let Jacob and Rosalie know what happened."

As she leaned over, Luke caught sight of the

locket she wore on her neck, and a sudden panic hit him full force.

My locket. I can't let Mr. Sir have my locket! Tiger. What has he done to my kitty? He said nothing, knowing his words would do no good.

As she drove, the social worker prattled on about where they were going and what was going to happen, but Luke paid no attention.

He could not get the locket and cat out of his mind.

Those two things were all that had mattered to the boy for many months. Even though he didn't recognize the woman pictured inside the locket, he had talked to that face as if it were his mother. The lady's smile had comforted him and soothed his fears. The only other woman who had ever made him feel that safe was Rosie.

A tear escaped and slid down Luke's face, but he made no move to wipe it away.

A half hour later, the social worker parked outside a house on the east side of Lancaster. Luke looked around before getting out of the car, hoping to see something familiar that would tell him where he was. All the houses looked exactly alike, including the one they were walking up to. Once they were close, Luke could see the house was not very pretty. Paint flaked off the windowsills and front door, and the siding was dirty.

The social worker hesitated before knocking, but seemed reassured when a smiling woman answered her knock. The short, plump lady, with orange hair and thick black-rimmed glasses that perched halfway down her pug nose, was eager with her greeting. "Welcome," she said, and then ushered the two inside.

The furnishings were sparse, but the house was clean and neat, and after a few minutes of conversation, the social worker left. The woman, who explained that her name was Mrs. Smathers, walked with Luke down a long hall, reciting rules of the house as she went.

Luke heard little of what she said. The room where she left him had two beds and a dresser. Both beds were neatly made and Mrs. Smathers pointed to one. Without a word, Luke crawled on top of the blankets and turned away from the woman, his head to the wall.

"Lunch is at noon. I suppose since you've hurt yourself, you are excused from chores this afternoon. Your roommate's name is Tom. He comes home from school at three thirty. I'm sure the two of you will get along splendidly. We don't allow fighting in this house…"

She was still talking as she left, shutting the door behind her.

***

Luke slept fitfully. He couldn't get the kitten or the locket out of his mind. After an hour of tossing and turning, his eyes flew open. He stared at a crack in the ceiling for many minutes, listening to a clock ticking somewhere in the house.

Suddenly, Luke heard a train's whistle. He sat up and listened. It didn't sound far away. With a look of determination, Luke jumped off the bed and went to the window. Carefully, slowly, he lifted the window with his good arm, trying to make no noise. He put one leg over the sill, then the other, and jumped, landing in the soft grass.

Luke looked around. He had no idea which way to go, but the train had triggered his action. He stood and tilted his head until he heard the whistle again.

Could he find his way back to the building where Tiger and his locket were? Could he find his way to the mall, and from there, to his building? He knew his bedroom was by the tracks because he'd often lain in bed listening to the trains pass, wishing he could get on one and go somewhere else.

Luke headed in the direction of the whistle. He was careful to stay off the main road—he didn't want anyone to see him. Instead, he dodged from yard to yard until he came to an open field and eventually, the raised tracks.

He stood on top of the tracks, hands on hips, and turned his face one way and then the other. Shrugging his shoulders, Luke set out.

Chapter 33

Rosalie sobbed into her hands, her whole body shaking. Jacob wanted to put his arms around her, but hesitated. He was uncomfortable lending comfort and didn't think it would do any good. Instead, he sat stiffly by her side in the waiting area of the hospital, patting her lap, and occasionally encircling her shoulder with a squeeze from his arm.

The joy from the last few days of entertaining a small boy had dissipated, gone in a matter of minutes when the two of them had returned to the hospital, bundles of new clothes in their arms, only to find an empty hospital bed. The nurse that had fretted over Luke explained that a woman from Social Services had taken Luke away, leaving no information on where they were going, just a business card.

The couple hadn't realized they'd have to deal with a system that didn't allow them to just take the child into their homes. Rules were rules and Mrs. Edna Thompson—as her business card read—was not about to be swayed by a nurse. Rosalie and Jacob had already convinced themselves that little Luke would be a part of their lives and now they didn't even know where he was or what to do about it. Mrs. Thompson was not answering her phone.

Instead of everything falling into place, it had fallen apart. Rosalie had been crying for fifteen minutes and Jacob felt completely inept at helping her get past the initial grief. He'd resorted to calling Rosalie's mom, hoping the mother could get through to her own child.

Mrs. McGovern had come right away, finding the couple lingering in the waiting area, unable to move forward while they let the situation sink in. But Rosalie's mom had been of little help. She'd wrung her hands, speaking of God and how he would take care of things. Her words fell on deaf ears. Rosalie didn't care about anything at the moment but the loss of Luke, and now Jacob not only had a crying Rosalie to attend to, but also her mother, who was hammering him with, "You have to do something. She can't go on this way. Get the doctor to give her a tranquilizer or something!"

Jacob couldn't think straight. He didn't recognize that part of what he was feeling was loss. He hadn't been raised to deal with emotion. He had no idea how to deal with a weeping woman, much less a nagging mom.

When Sam walked into the hospital's lobby/waiting room, he found a sobbing woman, a fretting mother, and a stiff-backed man, all sitting together.

"What on earth is going on?" Sam asked. "Has Luke taken a turn for the worse?"

His words got through to Rosalie; she stopped sobbing long enough to sniff and said in a weak voice, "They took him, Sam. They took him away from us."

"And who are they?" Sam asked, his curiosity now piqued. Did the little boy have family?

"The Social Services people," Rosalie's squeaky voice got out.

Jacob sat up even straighter, gaining his composure long enough to explain. He looked at the card he was holding. "Mrs. Edna Thompson from the Lancaster County Children and Youth Agency collected Luke and signed him out."

"Where did she take him?" Sam wanted to know.

"We don't know. She wouldn't say, and I haven't been able to get in touch with her. But the doctor signed off on his release."

With that pronouncement, Rosalie's crying resumed, her shoulders shaking, her head bowed to her hands.

Sam crossed his arms and looked at the couple—first Jacob, then Rosalie. In a voice that was gruff and unusually stern for the detective, he said, "Stop the bawling, Rosalie. It's accomplishing nothing!"

The words got everyone's attention. All three of their faces turned toward Sam.

A little more gently, Sam added, "Tears at this point are doing no good whatsoever. It's not time for grief. It's time for action."

As quickly as the tears had begun, they dried up. Rosalie took a handkerchief Jacob held out and wiped her eyes. She stood and straightened her clothes. Jacob stood beside her and put his arm around her shoulders. Mrs. McGovern just gaped at the rude detective from her perch on the sofa.

However, all three were now calm. Someone had finally taken charge.

"You're right, of course, Sam," said Jacob.

"So what do we do?" Rosalie asked softly.

"We'll start by having my assistant Casey make some calls and see if we can get this straightened out," Sam said to the three. "It will probably take some time, but I'm sure if we work with Social Services, we can get this going in a positive direction. Are you interested in taking guardianship?"

"Yes," Rosalie and Jacob said at the exact same moment. They looked at each other then, startled, but pleased, and reached for one another's hand.

The question had gotten Mrs. McGovern off her seat. "What? You're taking charge of that little thief! Together?"

Rosalie turned to her mother. She didn't let go of Jacob's hand.

"Yes, mother. We haven't worked out the details yet, but we both want to help Luke."

Rosalie then turned towards Sam. "Okay, Sam. What can we do?"

"Let's go home for now and tomorrow we'll get together and I'll tell you what I learned in Harrisburg and what Casey finds out from Social Services. Luke will be fine with these people for a while."

Jacob and Rosalie smiled weakly and nodded their heads. Mrs. McGovern grabbed her handbag and announced that she was late for a church meeting and would see Rosalie at home that night.

The couple and Sam agreed on a time to meet, and Sam left.

Rosalie and Jacob, still holding hands, walked out of the hospital to the parking lot. At Jacob's car, they paused. Jacob turned away to unlock the door; before opening it he paused and whispered, "I'm sorry."

Rosalie put a hand on his shoulder and turned him back toward her.

"It's not your fault they took him, Jake."

Jacob's face reflected shame. "That's not what I was apologizing for, Rosie. You fell apart and I couldn't handle it. I went back into my shell and was completely useless."

Rosalie shook her head. "No, no, no. It's me who should be apologizing. One little crisis and I reverted to 'poor, single, overweight Rosalie.' And Mother, as usual, was no help. I've got to get out of her house, Jake. I don't think I'll ever be able to take being in her constant presence."

"She means well…"

"Oh, I know this isn't her fault. She is who she is. But you and I, we have some work to do on ourselves if we want to take on the responsibility of another human being."

The car door was open. Rosalie started to get in on the driver's side. Jacob stopped her.

"I'll drive, Rosie. I need the practice."

In the car, the two were silent, thinking about all that had happened, and all that was to come.

***

At Mrs. McGovern's house, Jacob walked Rosalie to the door. She put her hand on the knob briefly and then turned back towards Jacob to find him standing very close. She looked deep into his eyes and saw love, but also something else. A fire she knew was deep within him that hadn't come to the surface except briefly during the few times they'd kissed.

Suddenly, their bodies were entwined. Rosalie's back was pressed against the door. Jacob's hands were in her hair. Their lips were crushed together.

By the time Jacob came to his senses and broke the hold of their passion, both were breathing heavily. He took a step back from her.

"I don't really know what comes over me when you're so close to me, Rosie. I know there is a time and place for this, and it probably isn't at your own front door. I hope your mother got to her meeting and hasn't seen us here."

Rosalie only laughed.

"I wish she had seen us, even if it meant the third degree for the rest of today. I think it's time she started getting used to the idea of us."

Jacob smiled at her comment and the warmth he had felt at the hospital when she'd called him "darling" returned. He loved the idea of an "us."

"Let's go to dinner tonight and make some plans, Rosie. I'll go get a couple of hours of work in and pick you up at seven?"

Rosalie reached out to touch his cheek. "Yes, my love, let's do."

In the car, any residual gloom from the hospital fell to the side and Jacob couldn't stop smiling. He knew Sam was right; action is what was needed, and he was determined to try his best to get Luke back. He also realized that he needed Sam's help again, or maybe Mrs. Wells. He needed to start shopping for an engagement ring.

Chapter 34

The next morning, Sam woke up at nine; surprised he'd slept so late, but refreshed and ready to tackle the day.

Casey's smile as he walked into the office suite was like a splash of refreshing water washing away the last vestiges of sleep.

"Want me to order you some breakfast from the deli next door?" she asked Sam.

"I had a bagel upstairs," he told her. He walked through her office and into his, Casey's wheelchair following him.

When he was seated, he glanced down at his open calendar and back up at his assistant.

"We're meeting with Jacob and Rosalie at eleven to report what we've learned about the steps they have to take in order to gain guardianship. I'm also going to report what I learned about the statues on my trip. In the meantime, I've got some follow up work for you on what I looked into yesterday." He handed her a file.

"Forget everything else I've got you working on and concentrate on this new info. I think we're close to finding the man behind these thefts."

"I'll get right on it, chief," Casey teased and

then turned her chair to depart, pulling his office door shut behind her.

Minutes later, Sam finished his coffee and set his cup in its place on his desk. He got up to walk and think. Suddenly, he grabbed his notes and went to the whiteboard.

He stared at the names he had put there, and picked up a dry marker eraser and took off two names. Sam had concluded that Laughlin Cosby, the man who had purchased the statues after they had been stolen at the Hardy residence, had no connection with the case other than buying the statues—Cosby had not known they were stolen. Jacob's art dealer Gregory Sterling, despite being a nasty man to deal with, was also a legitimate businessman. However, Gregory's nephew John Sterling, who often tracked down potential clients for his uncle and matched buyers with sellers for Sterling and Company, was an integral part of the thefts. He knew about Jacob's original purchases of the statues and had hooked Cosby up to buy the statues after they were stolen, unbeknownst to his uncle. John was not the Mr. Sir who masterminded the thefts, however. He had no access to the house or direct connection with Jacob.

Sam sat on a chair and leaned back to think about what he knew of Mr. Sir. The man was familiar enough with the Hardy home to find the doggy door. He also had access to the building where Luke had been kept, which had to be within a few miles of the Hardy home. Jacob and Rosalie had found out from Luke that Mr. Sir had driven an old truck a fairly short distance to and from the mansion, dropping the boy off and arranging to pick him up at the same spot after the thefts. When Sam asked Luke about the building itself, the boy had described climbing a set of stairs to get to a room with a bed and a working sink and little else except shelving and cupboards. Luke also mentioned that vagrants, or homeless people, occasionally stayed on the first floor of the building and that he wasn't allowed on the third floor, which was locked. Sam guessed the place was either an abandoned office building or an old factory—not a residence—and that the third floor was used to stow the goods Mr. Sir collected. That meant Mr. Sir either owned a building or rented space to have access to Luke's room and the third floor. From his discussions with Luke, Sam also noted that the building was near a railroad track because the boy described hearing trains on a frequent basis. It was within walking distance of a mall and a park where the boy spent his "free" time.

Sam had listed in his instructions to Casey for her to look for abandoned buildings in town, close to train tracks and a major shopping center, with a nearby park. There couldn't be too many places like that, because Lancaster didn't have many industrial areas that weren't in full use.

Sam stood, returning to his whiteboard, and wiped off 'Malcolm Sherburne.' The man was definitely doing something illegal with Jacob's characters and plots, but he had little reason to steal statues. He didn't stand to make nearly as much profit from the risky thefts as he might by making use of Jacob's books. He also didn't fit Luke's physical description of Mr. Sir. Malcolm was guilty of many sleazy things, but he was not Mr. Sir.

That left three possibilities: Kevin—and therefore Catherine—Wells, groundskeeper/handyman Horace Montgomery, or someone not yet identified.

Sam didn't really believe either Kevin or Catherine was involved and knew Kevin could not have pulled off the thefts without his wife's help. However, Sam wouldn't cross them off until he had better proof. Horace did not come across as either a mastermind, or a person wealthy enough to own a building, yet these three were the only ones that had regular access to the house and grounds.

Sam leaned back in his chair, closed his eyes, and tried to think things through, but as sometimes happened, his mind returned to his own past. How could anyone mistreat a small boy? Sam couldn't help wondering.

God, how he missed his son Davie. After all these years, Sam still sometimes woke from a deep sleep half expecting Davie to come bouncing into the room, landing on his chest, a bundle of giggles and energy. It had been fourteen years since he'd seen his son, but the hurt never seemed to dull.

"I wonder what he looks like now," Sam whispered to himself. "Does he resemble Barbara, or me? Would I know him if I saw him?"

Sam stood up, shaking his limbs and rotating his head and shoulders in an attempt to force his mind away from feeling the loss of his son.

Casey knocked and entered Sam's office, her grin wider than normal. "I think I found the location you're looking for. There's an area outside the Spring-fair Mall that has a row of abandoned factories and is close to the Penn railroad tracks. I'll check with the county assessment office to see if any of the buildings are connected with our suspects."

The phone interrupted Casey's report. Sam picked it up and barked, "Sam Osborne here."

On the other end of the line was Jacob Hardy, his voice shaky and panicked. "Luke is gone," he gasped. "They can't find him anywhere!"

"Calm down, Jacob. What do you mean he's gone? Gone from where? When did this happen?"

"He disappeared sometime yesterday from the foster home where they took him—no one knows exactly when, though it was sometime before the school kids got home at three thirty."

"Who discovered this? How did you find out?"

Sam heard Jacob take a deep breath. "A lady from the home where they took Luke called me a few minutes ago. The police have been looking for him, but they've had no luck. Social Services thought he might have found his way back to my house, but they took their sweet time coming to that conclusion! He's been gone all night."

The panic returned to Jacob's voice. "Oh God, do you think Mr. Sir has him? What can we do? How can we find him? What will that creep do to our little boy?"

Chapter 35

Once Sam had contacted Social Services and the police department for updates, he drove to the Hardy home. He didn't need to knock on the door, or even ring the doorbell; Jacob opened it before Sam was up the last step.

"Did you find him?" Jacob asked, while almost pulling Sam into the house.

"Not yet, Jacob. I did get the location of the home the agency took him to, so grab your coat and we'll go talk to the woman together."

Rosalie came around from behind Jacob and grabbed Sam's upper arm. "I'm coming too." It was apparent by her red eyes that she had been crying again. "We have to find him—it's cold outside."

"Rosie, he'll know to stay warm. He's used to taking care of himself," Sam said. "I know you want to do what's best, so I need you to stay at Jacob's. I don't know if he has the capability to find his way here without help, but this is one place he might go. You need to be here in case he shows up."

Sam gently extracted Rosalie's fingers from his sleeve. "I know this is hard, Rosie. But I assure you, we'll find Luke. The police have been alerted and are on the watch for a stray boy. They'll help us find him."

***

Mrs. Emily Smathers sounded sincere in her concern and anxiety over what had happened to Luke.

"The little guy seemed exhausted when he got here, so I put him to bed, intending to wake him for the noontime meal. But I'm afraid I got busy. The other children are off at school, so I took the opportunity of the quiet to get some laundry done and watch my soaps. But I swear, I intended to get him up at one or so and feed him a sandwich and then introduce him around when the kids got home.

"I was shocked when I went to fetch him at probably 1:30 and found the open window."

Mrs. Smathers was wringing her hands.

"I'm afraid I got very little notice that he was coming and I wasn't at my best when he arrived. I hope I didn't scare the boy off."

Sam saw a trace of tears in the woman's eyes.

"I've never lost a wee one before. Never. He's so small. If he gets hurt, it will be my fault."

Sam cleared his throat. "Mrs. Smathers, you didn't have him in your care long enough for this to be your fault. Luke simply saw an opportunity to get away. You couldn't have known that a small boy who had just checked out of the hospital would have the foresight, or desire, to run away."

The conversation was interrupted by a knock on the door. Casey's husband Danny from the Lancaster police force had responded to Sam's plea for help. Danny, Sam, and a fellow officer Danny had brought along, tracked the boy's footprints through several yards, but the tracks disappeared at a sidewalk. The police officers questioned neighbors and some of the shop personnel from a few blocks away, but no one had seen the boy.

"Where could he be?" Jacob kept asking Sam, as they accompanied the officers canvassing the neighborhood. Jacob had stopped along the way several times to call Rosalie, but she had nothing to report.

"He wouldn't have gone back to where he was living, or to Mr. Sir, would he, Sam? He seemed terrified of the man."

"I wouldn't think so, Jacob, unless there was something there he needed."

Jacob's eyes widened with alarm.

"What, Jacob?" Sam asked.

"He talked about a cat, Sam, after he started to get comfortable with Rosie and me. We were keeping him busy, playing Go Fish, and he held up one of the cards that had a picture of a kitten. He stared at it for a moment and said something about hoping the kitty could find some mice. We questioned him about it, but he didn't seem to want to talk about it, so we let it drop. However, when he talked about how scared of Mr. Sir he was, Luke mentioned threats the man made against both of them—both Luke and the cat. Do you suppose Luke is trying to get back to his pet? Oh God, what will Mr. Sir do if the boy goes back there?”

Jacob was in full panic mode now, so Sam tried logic.

“He’s a little boy who walked away from a new location in Lancaster. It’s very unlikely he’d even know which way to go to find his way back. He probably hasn’t gotten that far. The police are sure to spot him, or someone will report him.”

Sam tilted his head.

“Listen.” He brought his finger to his lips to stop their conversation. In the distance, Sam, Jacob, and the officers heard the wail of a train whistle.

Sam’s face lit up. He opened his cell phone and called Casey. “Tell me what you learned about where the vacant buildings are.”

He nodded his head and murmured into the phone, taking notes as he talked. Then he closed his cell and spoke to the police officers, and then Jacob. Sam and Jacob got in one car, Danny and his fellow officer got into another, and the two cars took off at full speed, the siren of the police car blazing. They were headed to the home of Horace Montgomery.

They were met there by another patrol car and the officers approached the home. No one answered the door, but knowing they had probable cause to think the boy was in danger, the officers found an unlocked back door and entered the home, searching from top to bottom. There was no sign of Luke or Horace.

Sam stood in the yard, his phone in his ear, getting more information from Casey. This time, when he hung up, he rattled off a street address to the police officers and turned to Jacob. "The building where he was held, it's not far from here. We should have gone there first!"

One patrol car stayed behind while Sam and Jacob, Danny, and his fellow officer ran to their cars. Danny punched the address into his GPS and his patrol car led the way this time as the cars took off, paying little attention to speed limits.

Chapter 36

The rescue party saw a truck parked between two buildings at the address that Danny's GPS led them to, a site close to the railroad tracks. They didn't know exactly which building was the one Horace's father had once run as a successful machine shop. Both structures appeared abandoned and neglected. To cover more ground, the two police officers split up; one going with Jacob, one with Sam. The officers led the way, their guns drawn.

Sam and Danny took the building on the left, Danny's firearm leading the way. The two men spoke in low voices as they found an unlocked door and crept inside. They had barely gotten inside the door when they heard voices.

"Give me the damn locket, boy. You owe it to me!"

"No," squeaked a boy's voice.

"Give me the damn locket or I'll wring this critter's scrawny neck!"

"Let Tiger go and I'll give it to you," Luke sobbed.

Danny and Sam moved forward through a cavernous dark room toward the sound of the voices coming from the back. As they got closer, they saw a flight of steps leading to a small room raised up on a platform that at one time had probably been an office for a supervisor. A big picture window faced the expanse of the former shop floor and was caked with grime and dirt, letting only a few shafts of light through.

The two men crept across the floor towards the office, hoping they couldn't be seen out of the grimy window. A door stood ajar at the front of the raised office and Sam motioned for Danny to go to the other side of the raised area, where another set of steps led to a second door. Sam crouched and approached the open front door from an angle that he hoped would prevent him from being seen by those inside the small room.

"That locket is mine, boy and you stole it."

"I didn't steal it, Mr. Sir," Luke sniffed. "I had it when I came here."

Jacob and Danny heard the door behind them creak open. Their fellow rescuers had completed their search of the other building. Sam prayed Horace and Luke couldn't hear the creaking from across the giant floor space. He continued inching up the steps toward the open office door.

"Everything in this damn building is mine, boy. And that includes this here cat and your damn locket! You owe me big time, you worthless piece of shit. You cost me a pretty penny."

Sam was now at the top of the steps and close enough to peer into the room. He saw a red-faced Horace holding a kitten by the scruff with one hand and Luke by the throat with the other. The small boy was gasping for breath while reaching towards the kitten, his feet dangling. A chain and locket hung from his bandaged arm.

"I ought to beat the living daylights out of you, boy."

Danny, who had crept up to the other door, raised his gun, preparing to enter the room from the side.

Sam saw Horace drop the boy to the hard cement floor and then throw the cat towards the door Sam was about to enter. The pet was momentarily stunned, but managed to scamper away.

Sam's eyes met Horace's at the same moment Danny opened the side door. However, Horace's gaze only fixed momentarily on Sam and then landed on something past Sam's head, eyes widening with surprise. Sam felt a shove from behind him as a body hurled forward and plowed head first into Horace's chest. Sam heard a whoosh of air leaving Horace's lungs.

"Run, Luke, run!" Jacob screamed as he and Horace fell to the ground. Luke crawled on hands and knees towards the open front door, while Danny rushed forward from the side, aiming his gun at Horace.

Horace Montgomery laid face down for a moment moaning in pain, and then he turned over to stare up into the face of a man he'd never imagined could take him down. Jacob's eyes were slits, his breath labored.

"Don't you ever touch that boy again—Mr. Sir," Jacob growled as he sat astride Horace.

Jacob seemed to get control of his anger and struggled to his feet. He kept one foot firmly planted on Horace's chest to keep the man in place.

"I swear to you, Horace Montgomery, that you will pay for every day you've held that boy here in this building and for every time you've made him a thief. I intend to see you in prison for a long time."

"Well, I'll be damned," Horace whistled softly as he lay gazing up at the stranger Jacob had become. "I guess you have some of your old man in you after all."

Chapter 37

Rosalie expertly balanced a tray of tall glasses of lemonade and a plate of cookies. She set the tray down on the coffee table and then situated herself on the couch beside Jacob. The two smiled warmly at each other.

"Where's Luke?" Sam interrupted the couple to ask. Jacob and Rosalie turned towards Sam's voice.

"Safely ensconced in what we're calling his room, watching television, his faithful kitty at his side. He's utterly fascinated with the TV." Rosalie chuckled. "I'm afraid I'm going to have to limit his time with that box."

"He's got some catching up to do on the cartoons," Sam said, visualizing a time in his life when he sat with his son on his lap, sharing the silliness of Sponge Bob Squarepants.

Sam sighed and reached over for a glass, taking a large sip of the cold refreshment. "Delicious lemonade, Rosalie. Thanks." He set the glass back down on a coaster and wiped the condensation off the rim. "I've got a lot to report. Some of it won't please you."

"There's not a lot you could say after all this that will upset us, Sam," Rosalie said. She glanced down at the large diamond that glistened on her finger.

"I'm just glad to get this all out in the open," Jacob added.

Sam sat back on the large easy chair and looked from Jacob to Rosalie, awed at how drastic a change love had made in these two individuals. They were now collaborating on the book writing, with Rosalie acting as full advisor on plots and characters, but leaving the actual writing to the talented author. A judge had granted Jacob temporary custody of Luke.

"Let's start with your agent, Malcolm Sherburne," Sam said. "I know I asked if you'd ever signed over movie rights to the man. Could he have tricked you into signing a document you didn't study closely, Jacob?"

Jacob's face reddened and Sam wasn't sure if it was from embarrassment or anger.

"I am quite certain I never signed legal documentation that gave him permission to use my books in any way other than to market the print versions. I read all my contracts thoroughly. And I have no desire to see the books I've written up on a movie screen."

Sam reached for a cookie and took a big bite, seeking a bit of sweetness before he had to share the rest of the sourness with Jacob.

"I didn't think so," he said. "However, Malcolm has had a little side business going for most of the last five years. I guess the hundreds of thousands of dollars he made off your books wasn't quite enough for him, because he's been taking the plots and characters and turning them into porn movies."

The red in Jacob's face deepened as he reached for the sofa arm and squeezed.

Sam continued, "I crossed Malcolm off the list of suspects early on because he had no need to steal your statues. But I'm afraid his greed got the better of him."

"What he's done is surely illegal!" Rosalie said.

"The movie-making itself is not strictly illegal, though he's been dragged in once for being present at a film-making session not approved by the owner of the building where it was happening. But it's likely a copyright infringement, if you can prove he's used your books. I'm afraid it will be up to you and your counsel to seek charges, unless you can get local law enforcement to bring it before the prosecutor, Jacob. You're the wronged party here and you may well have a right to civil damages."

Sam took another bite of cookie.

"That bastard," Jacob said through clenched teeth. "All these years I thought he had my interests in mind. In some ways, I thought of him as a friend."

"He's pretty convincing as a jolly old man," Sam commented. "And his job was to make you feel good—confident that you were writing what people would pay money to read. I guess in that way, he was being honest. He did know how to make your books popular."

Jacob shook his head back and forth.

"That doesn't forgive his betrayal and greed," he said softly. Rosalie reached for his hand.

Sam continued, his tone even as he gave more of his report.

"I'm not sure how Horace hooked up with Luke in the first place, but we all know now that your handyman coached the boy in stealing—not only here, but in several other houses where Horace was employed."

It was Rosalie's turn to be angry.

"How could he use Luke like that?"

Sam reached for his lemonade, took a sip, and then set it carefully back down on the coaster.

"Believe it or not, Luke's monumental reward was the huge sum of two dollars per statue, which the boy mostly saved for major things Horace didn't provide, such as shoes. As far as I can tell, all he provided was cheap cereal, an occasional hot meal, a lot of threats, a few thrashings and—once in a while—a bit of kindness; just enough to keep the boy there. It's pretty amazing how he controlled the boy. I'm not even sure Luke got money from the other thefts. I think he was paid for this job because your house was locked up like a fortress. Horace needed Luke to squeeze through that doggie door, which is how the boy got cut."

Sam set a second cookie down on his napkin and reached for his notebook before continuing.

"Your statues didn't actually net Horace that

much individually. Once he found a good buyer, it was enough to keep him going and he was able to ask more from his buyer with each acquisition. I actually believe this whole side business of stealing from clients started out slow, but like with Malcolm, greed took hold. I think that with the last theft, he was aiming for a big windfall. The police say he was about to take off for some tropical paradise to let things cool down for awhile and take advantage of his ill-gotten gains."

"How did you discover who it was?" Jacob asked.

"By degrees, as I do with most investigations," Sam answered. "Several days before I went to Harrisburg, I received a call from the police chief in Petersburg, Virginia. I sent pictures of the statues to many precincts in this area of the country asking them to be on the lookout. As it happens, one of the officers at the Petersburg department remembered spotting something similar in a store window in Richmond. By the time the police went to the store to investigate, the statue was gone. The store claimed it had no idea that the statue was stolen and with a little pressure from police, gave us the buyer's name—Laughlin Cosby in Harrisburg—so that we could authenticate whether he had your statues."

"Horace went all the way to Richmond to fence my statues?" Jacob asked, a look of puzzlement on his face. "Isn't that several hours away?"

"Yes, but he only had to make the trip the first time. The store, called Antiques and More, is owned by Gregory Sterling—the same man who originally sold you the statues. It's run by his nephew, John Sterling, who lives here in Lancaster."

"So Gregory Sterling was in on this?" Rosalie asked, a look of surprise on her face. "How could he even think he'd get away with it? Was he in cahoots with Horace?"

Sam smiled then and gently shook his head.

"Much as I wouldn't mind catching Gregory Sterling at something illegal just to cut his ego down a few notches, the dealer had nothing to do with the robberies, or the movement of your statues, though his store may be legally liable for the first sale."

Rosalie and Jacob looked at each other, confused.

"Mr. Sterling's nephew John Sterling is already sitting in jail—turned in by his own uncle. John made the first sale from the store and then proceeded on his own. He knew the value of Jacob's statues from his uncle. John is the buyer for that store in Petersburg. He also has a handy little business pawning stolen goods. He was well aware the statues were stolen when he bought them from Horace and sold them to Mr. Cosby. John was the broker in the whole deal."

"But how did he connect with Horace?" Jacob wanted to know.

"It seems this is not the first time the pair has done business. Some of Horace's other stolen goods have been sold through John. The two have been in cahoots for some time."

"And Gregory Sterling is just now discovering this?" Rosalie asked.

"The fine arts part of Horace's business has only been going on for about a year and a half. In fact, our little thief upstairs in front of the TV has experience stealing jewelry, cash, and other small items from Horace's customers. Horace's usual procedure was to canvas a place through his handyman work, wait for the owners to be out of the house or asleep, and then work together with his little accomplice.

"He probably would not have attempted this job if he had not discovered the statues' worth and found the doggie door. It was a crime of opportunity and by this time he had already started selling more valuable items to John Sterling."

Sam closed his notebook. "Anyway, I'm sure you're relieved it didn't turn out to be Catherine or her husband. Catherine's greatest crime is chatting about the statues to Horace and then showing them to both Horace and her husband. Kevin, as you know, has already suffered for crimes not committed."

Sam patted his mouth with a napkin, and then stood, ready to return to his office and another case.

Jacob and Rosalie rose to their feet.

"I have every intention of keeping Kevin and Catherine on for a long time, Sam," Jacob said.

Sam nodded his head, a pleased smile on his face. He looked from Jacob to Rosalie.

"I know you have a battle ahead of you, clearing Luke of his part in this crime, and getting proper custody of him. I have confidence you'll succeed with a good lawyer and a fair judge. The boy has never been given a chance to learn what's wrong and what's right, but I sense he has a good heart."

Rosalie and Jacob nodded their heads in agreement. Sam turned to leave, but turned back.

"Oh, and Laughlin Cosby is ready to return those statues, Jacob. He'll be reimbursed either by the lawsuit he intends to file against Gregory Sterling's business or by an insurance company, and he also knows they hold sentimental value to you. I've given him your number and he'll be calling."

Jacob put his arm around Rosalie. "As far as I'm concerned, he can him keep them. They've lost any fascination for me. I have what I need right here."

Epilogue

One Year Later

The small boy flew down the stairs, backpack trailing him, sneakers squeaking to a stop at the bottom.

"Slow down, Luke. You mustn't run down those stairs. We wouldn't want you to get hurt on this special day," Jacob said to his son.

The boy dropped his pack and turned round and round, stopping to pose each time he faced Jacob and Rosalie. "Look at me! Look at me! Aren't I grand?" Luke asked, a huge smile lighting his face.

"Indeed you are," Rosalie said, stepping forward and hugging him close to her breast.

"Will I look like the other kids? Do they have new sneakers as well?" His brow wrinkled with concern.

"Oh, yes," Rosalie assured him. "Many parents buy their kids new clothes for the first day of school. You'll fit right in."

"But I'm older than the kids in my class. Will they think I'm dumb?"

"They won't know how old you are until you're ready to tell them, Luke," Jacob said. "And no, you are hardly dumb! You're one of the smartest boys I know and you have many stories to tell the others about the last year, going to court and putting criminals behind bars."

"Besides, Luke, you've grown a lot in this last year and you're about the same size as the other kids in your class," Rosalie added. "Just smile your wonderful smile, and you'll have a bunch of friends very soon. They will love you almost as much as Jacob and I do." She bent down to kiss the top of his head.

***

The trio got into the car and drove to school. Soon enough, Luke would be riding the bus with the other children. However, he hadn't been to school in several years and despite how far he'd come with tutoring, he wasn't used to a school environment.

Jacob and Rosalie had arranged to take him into the classroom before the bell rang. They had already met his teacher, Mrs. Olson, and when they walked into her schoolroom, she was waiting for them, her smile warm and welcoming.

After a few pleasantries, Jacob and Rosalie bid their goodbyes and left. Mrs. Olson had already engaged Luke in helping with last minute adjustments to the classroom. He wasn't looking at his parents when they left.

In the hall, Rosalie allowed tears to fall as she felt the giant pit in her gut that parents feel when they first cut the daily bind they have with their children.

Jacob took her hand and once outside began

to talk in a low voice.

"See the kids get off the bus Rosalie? He'll fit right in. I'm sure of it."

Rosalie looked up, wiped away her tears, and watched the roughhousing; the already messy mix of arms and legs, new clothes, flying hair, smiles and singsong chatter. She realized he was probably right. Luke was just another elementary school child who needed to be among people his age.

Jacob opened her car door and then went around to his side.

Seated behind the wheel, he turned to his new bride.

"Rosalie, you know it's right for Luke to attend public school. He needs the socialization with the other kids. He needs to know how most kids live their lives."

Jacob sat back and sighed. "Lord knows I could have used it."

That got Rosalie's attention. She wiped away the rest of her sadness with a one-handed rub of her face, looking over at her husband.

"You didn't go to a public school?"

Jacob still had not started the car. He turned from his wife towards the dashboard, rested his hands on the wheel, and bowed his head, his mind traveling back forty years.

"Oh, yeah, I was in school. For exactly one

week!"

Rosalie could see that Jacob was upset, "What happened, Jake?"

He turned to look at her. "It's funny. I started out hating that week. While the other kids wore bright-colored, wide-collared shirts and casual pants, I was dressed in a black suit and skinny tie, my hair slicked down with this awful grease. They called me the funeral director."

"Kids can be cruel," Rosalie said.

"I know. But by the second day, I'd relaxed and begun to enjoy what the teacher was teaching. The kids tired of teasing and by the end of the week, I'd made a friend on the playground."

"Then what happened?" Rosalie asked in a soft voice.

"Well," Jacob said, his eyes returning to gaze out the front window. "I made the fatal mistake of falling off the jungle gym and scraping my knee."

"Were you hurt badly?"

Jacob laughed softly and shook his head.

"Not physically really. It was just a bad scrape. But the school had to send home an incident report and when my parents saw it, that was all it took. Dad was angry and Mom was frightened, which was how I spent a good portion of my childhood!"

His eyes returned to Rosalie. "After that, I was homeschooled by tutors and I never saw my friend again. Can't even remember her real name—she called me Prince Suit and Tie and I called her Princess Fluff."

Suddenly, Rosalie sat up very straight.

"All I remember," Jacob continued, "was that she'd lost her dad that year and she carried around a good luck charm—a silver dollar her dad had given her. He said if she buried it, it would grow a lifetime of luck for her, but she hadn't been able to part with it. On my last day of school, before I hurt my knee, we buried it together under the monkey bars."

He turned to find her gaping at him.

"Was the little girl fat?" she asked.

"No. At least I don't remember her that way."

"Did you call her Princess Fluff because she wore dresses with lots of taffeta and bows?"

Jacob cocked his head to think for a second. "Yeah, I think she did. And she had curly black hair and wore glasses."

Rosalie reached over and took one of Jacob's hands off the wheel. "It didn't work," she said.

Jacob drew his brows together in confusion. "What didn't work?"

"The lifetime of luck."

All at once, it dawned on Jacob what she was saying. "It was you!"

Rosalie's whole face was lit up with amazement. "I always wondered where my new friend went," she said. "It was only a few days at an early age, but it made a big impression on me. You'll never know how much that little ceremony under the monkey bars helped me get over my father and get on with my life. "

She leaned forward then and forgetting they were still in a school parking lot, gave him a powerful, love-laden kiss.

When they drew away from each other, they were not out of breath, just happy and warm. Jacob finally started the car. Before he could back out of the space, he heard Rosalie's voice.

"Well, come to think of it, maybe it did work. It just took awhile for the luck tree to germinate."

CPSIA information can be obtained at www.ICGtesting.com
Printed in the USA
LVOW13s0248100314

376705LV00004B/358/P